Friends, Lovers, Strangers

Corine Leon

Prologue

"Let him go." The tall boy breathed, looking down at the lanky kid that had a smaller and very uncomfortable looking boy held in an uncomfortable position. Although he was trying to appear brave, behind those ugly glasses of his, his owl-like eyes were very close to tears.

"Mind your business, Matt." The lanky kid spat out, holding the kid tighter by the scruff of his shirt, causing his eyes to bulge out.

"I'm not going to repeat myself, Wet Pants Boy." The taller boy said slowly, a mischievous glint in his eyes and a satisfied smirk on his face. Immediately, the bully let go of the bespectacled boy, looking around to see if anyone heard what the other boy said. In a normal world, maybe no one would have minded the three kids; no one would have paid them any attention. But the middle school playground was no ordinary place and kids find entertainment everywhere.

"That wasn't me. I didn't do it!" the bully spluttered, growing redder by the moment while the taller boy looked on, humor and mischief dancing like twin flames in his eyes.

"Did too! The pants don't lie."

"Shut up, Matt!" the bully boy said and ran off, eliciting bouts of giggles from the onlookers.

"Show is over, freaks. Go find something else to laugh at." Matt, the taller boy said but not before he stopped for a few seconds to bask in the glow of his victory.

Not to direct his wrath at them lest he knows about some of their rather unpleasant secrets, the kids all turned away and it was business as usual again.

"Jason, are you okay?" Matt asked the bespectacled boy who was still trying to compose himself.

"Yeah, Matt. Thank you for coming to my rescue. Again." He said the last bit drily but not without affection.

"It's no problem at all. Come on, let's go."

"Uhm, where are we going?" he asked his friend suspiciously. He had heard that voice before and he didn't like the sound of it. Not one bit. The last time he sounded like that, they ended up getting into trouble with the principal and their parents were almost called to the school. Matt's parents would have been used to such calls, but his parents would certainly have been surprised. They got really lucky that day.

"Relax. We are just going to meet Mel. We're going to carpool today, remember? Ice cream after school? You told me your parents said you could come." He shot him an accusatory look.

"Oh, yeah." Jason laughed shakily. "I thought you were going to get me in trouble again."

"What do you mean 'again'? I get you out of trouble, not into them."

"Really? Where should I begin? That first day at preschool with the gum…"

By the time the two boys arrived at their destination, Jason had ticked eight things off the list, using his fingers to count and Matt was looking decidedly glum.

"Why do you look like someone kicked you, Matt?" The last member of their group, Melissa asked in a singsong voice, suddenly appearing before them.

"Jason is being an ass." He replied in a glum voice.

"That's unusual. Usually, you're the ass." She answered, twirling one end of her long, blonde pigtail round her middle finger.

"You see!" Jason said, giving Melissa a nod of approval.

Matt looked between Jason and Melissa and turned away.

"I hate you guys."

"Oh come on, Matty! You know we love you."
Melissa said, running after him.

"That's true. We accept you and all your mischief."
Jason added.

They continued that way all the way to the parking
lot where Melissa's driver was waiting for them.

Chapter One

"Melissa, you're going to be late if you don't come down right now!" Melissa's mother shouted at her from the dining area. A few minutes later, Melissa thundered down the stairs and her mother's eyes widened in surprise.

"Good morning, mum." Melissa, ignoring her mother's look of surprise, dropped a kiss on her mother's cheek and proceeded to dive into her breakfast which had already been laid out for her.

"Father left already, I see." She said drily with her mouth full of pancakes and bacon.

"Don't talk with food in your mouth, young lady." Her mother said, finally getting over her initial surprise. "And don't sound like that. You know your father has a lot of business to attend to."

"Yeah, sure. Not like breakfast with his family, or even talking to his daughter makes it to top three on the list of the business he has to attend to."

"Melissa!"

For a few seconds, defiance and pity for her mother waged a war across her face, but in the end, pity won.

"I'm sorry." She whispered and went back to her food. Her father had never really been around, but in the past few months, he had been away even more than usual and Melissa could see the strain on her mother's face. She pretended not to, of course, just like she pretended not to hear their loud fights every time her father came home late. Which was every other day now. In a house as big as theirs, you can pretend not to hear two people raise their voices at each other and get away with it.

"It's okay, baby. You know I love you, right?" her mother asked suddenly, grabbing both of her hands in hers. For a few seconds, her eyes were wild, out of focus, as if she was thinking about multiple things at once and her brain was threatening to shut down. Melissa had never seen her usually well put together mum like that before and it took her aback.

"Yes, mum. I know, and I love you too."

"And you will tell me if there is anything bothering you? You know you can always talk to me, don't you?"

"Yes, mother. I know, but you are scaring me a little. Is everything alright?"

"I should be asking you that." She looked pointedly at her daughter's clothes and gothic makeup.

"Oh." Melissa said, looking away, "It's just something I'm trying." She sat back in her chair and moved her hands away from her mother's grip.

"Talk to me, baby." Her mother pleaded, with her eyes and her mouth.

Melissa sighed deeply and out of habit brought her long hair to hang down one shoulder. Playing with her hair is one of her many nervous habits.

"You dyed your hair pink!" her mother gasped.

"It's just the tip."

Her mother continued to stare at her with eyes filled with despair and Melissa kicked herself mentally for putting that look in her mother's eyes. It's bad enough that her father already did the same thing.

"Ryan broke up with me." She whispered, not taking her eyes off her plate.

"Oh, my love I'm so sorry." Her mother said, one hand on her chest.

"It's fine." Melissa said nonchalantly, or as nonchalantly as she could sound with tears threatening to leak from her eyes. She wiped the tears angrily, making a mess of her heavy makeup in the process. When she saw the part of her makeup that followed her hand away from her face, she burst into full blown tears.

When her first love had broken up with her a few days to resumption of their last year in high school, she had not cried. She didn't know how to process the emotions because what do you do when the person you trusted enough to keep all the parts that makes you who you are with tosses them out and says those parts are no longer at home with them? She didn't know then, so she did the first thing that came to her mind. She got a makeover. It took her mind off what she should have been processing and in a way; she thought that if she looked like someone else, it would all go away and she would wake up one day and find a text from Ryan telling her that he loved her. It was stupid and irrational and completely bonkers, but she was heartbroken and all those things seem to go hand in hand when you are heartbroken.

Sitting in the kitchen with her mother, feeling like a stranger in her own body, the reality of the situation hit her and she finally began to feel the enormity of heartbreak.

"I'm so sorry, honey." Her mother said, moving her chair closer to her so she could pull her into a hug. It was a classic case of not knowing you need something until it is offered to you as Melissa melted into her mother and allowed herself to cry.

"Do you want to take the day off from school?"

"No." she said after a while, sniffling "I need to keep my perfect attendance record."

Her mother smiled at her, remembering the story behind the perfect attendance record bit and it took her to the times when things were simple, when she sat at the table with her family and ate and laughed. The good, easy times.

"Okay, baby. You take your time. I'll call the principal to inform him that you'll be late."

"Thank you, mum." She sniffed and started crying again. She hadn't planned to tell her mum, or anyone for that mother. She had figured it would be like one of those breakup moments in movies where the girl takes it like a bad bitch and moves on with her life like nothing happened and the boy sees this and regrets his decision. At no point did it occur to her that she would have a breakdown in front of her mother with Goth makeup dripping down her face.

"This is so messed up." Melissa said between crying and laughing.

"Life is, baby. But I promise you, it gets better. There will be men that will hold you and never let go."

Melissa giggled and gave her mum a pointed look, understanding passing between them.

"I know what you're thinking, but you don't have to use your dad and I as a standard for what love should look like. I don't want you to make the mistakes I made."

"Oh?" Melissa said, looking confused. She had never heard her mum talk like this.

"I should have told you all these things but I kind of just let you grow on your own, didn't I? I'm sorry, my darling. I'll do better, I promise."

"It's okay."

"Do you want to wipe your make-up and let me drive you to school?"

"Yes, please. Shit. I don't know what I was thinking." She murmured to herself.

"Don't be too hard on yourself. You are allowed moments of imperfection, my darling."

Melissa stood up to leave. She turned around when she got to the kitchen entrance and started at her mother for a few seconds.

"Thank you." She turned around immediately and headed for her room.

Melissa had never been extremely close with her mother, but the moment they just shared gave her a completely different view of the woman and she realized that she might have been missing out on a lot.

"There is a blessing in every loss." Jason's voice drifted to her unbidden and she rolled her eyes. The damned boy just has to be right all the time.

Chapter Two

"Why do you think she's late? It's very unusual for her to come late to school." Jason asked nervously, adjusting his glasses for what has to be the hundredth time to Matt's annoyance.

"Geez, how I wish I can know things just from the unresponded texts I send out." Matt ground out and gave Jason a sour look.

"You don't have to be a douche, you know that. Right?"

"Shit." Matt ran his hands through his hair in a frustrated manner and turned to face Jason fully.

"I'm sorry, bro. I didn't mean to lash out like that."

"Wanna talk about it?"

"Not right now. I need to figure stuff out on my own first." He smiled nervously at his friend and Jason looked at him as if he had grown an extra head. Matt had never looked unsure a day in his life. Jason had no doubt he was born with that cocky look on his face.

"Are we cool?" Matt asked, his expression too sincere for Jason to refuse him forgiveness.

"Sure, man. And if you wanna talk about it…" "I know. I know."

The school bell rang, the first warning, in five minutes it will ring again and all students were expected to be in their classes.

"Shit. Do you think Mel is ditching school today?" Jason asked worriedly.

"That's highly unlikely. Remember how she came to school even when she had that flu because…" "She didn't want to spoil her perfect attendance record." Jason completed and Matt nodded in agreement.

"That's right. I don't think she's about to start now." "What do we do?" Jason asked him expectantly.

"No idea, and we have less than two minutes to decide."

They were saved from having to do anything when Melissa's mother drove into the school parking lot and a pink haired version of Melissa jumped down from the passenger's seat, waved frantically at her mum and started running towards the boys.

"Is that…?"

"Did she…?"

Matt and Jason started to say, but neither of them completed their sentences as their jaws chose to hang open instead.

"Come on, don't just stand there. We are going to be late for first period!" Melissa said as she ran past them, deliberately ignoring the look of surprise on their faces.

She turned around to see if they had followed her, they hadn't.

"Guys, are you coming?" she queried quizzically and they seemed to snap out of their reverie and started running after her.

They made it to English class in time, but only barely. The only available seats were at the back, and while Matt was very comfortable with sitting at the back, Melissa and Jason didn't like it.

"Great. Now I'm going to be stuck at the back of the class for the rest of the year." Jason grumbled. "I blame you for this." He shot daggers at Melissa and she rolled her eyes dramatically.

"Our chairs are not comfortable enough for your royal highnesses?" The English teacher asked, clearly pissed at something. Or someone.

"No, sir. We were just getting settled in. Happy resumption!" Melissa smiled sweetly at him and said in her best cheerleader voice. The teacher relaxed visibly and Melissa made a face at Jason before settling in next to Matt. Since he didn't have a choice, Jason took the seat next to Melissa and spent the rest of the class trying to make sure the teacher noticed his presence in the class.

Matt spent the rest of the class trying to pretend he was paying attention in class, while he was really just trying not to lean in closer to Melissa to drown in the intoxicating smell of her. He was usually able to control his reactions to her presence, but with everything that was happening at home, his mind was in about a thousand fractures and he was not able to exert the same amount of control that he used to.

He needed to distract himself, so he did the one thing people knew him for, he caused trouble.

Seemingly out of nowhere, a tight wad of paper sailed through the air and hit Mr. Finch, the English teacher square in the middle of his head.

"Okay, who did that?" Mr. Finch asked angrily, retrieving the weapon from the floor. Angrily, he began to unwrap the paper only to find a very graphic pornographic image scribbled crudely on it.

"I repeat, who did this?"

Before he could grill them any further, the bell rang and the students shot off from their seats like bullets and filed out without giving him a backward glance. By the time Melissa and her friends passed by him, he was fuming openly. Melissa offered him and apologetic smile and scurried off after her friends.

"You just had to do that, didn't you?" Jason said drily, cutting Matt a disapproving glare.

"I'm sorry, grandpa." Matt said, rolling his eyes at Jason. Jason's goody two shoes behavior sometimes got on his nerves.

"Cut it out, you guys." Melissa interrupted before the inevitable back and forth ensued.

"What's up with you?" Matt asked with a tenderness he reserved for only her, not like she knew that.

"More importantly, what's up with your hair? I've been dying to ask."

Sure enough, they were getting a lot of strange looks from the other students on the hallway, but no one approached them…yet.

"Later. Let's do lunch in our old spot?" she implored, her eyes wide and desperate.

"The roof? Isn't that place out of bounds now?" Jason asked.

"Sure, we'll be there." Matt said, staring pointedly at Jason and daring him to say anything.

"Okay."

"Thank you. I'll see you boys later."

With that, she turned and headed in the direction of her next class.

"Dude, I'm supposed to be the insensitive, clueless one in this group, but even I could see there is something big weighing her down."

"I know. I've just never seen her that way before, I'm not sure how to deal with it."

"There is nothing to deal with, it's not about you. We'll give her what she needs now."

"When did you become so smart? Did something happen to you over the holidays?" Before Matt could respond, Jason gasped. "Or were you abducted by body snatching aliens? Who are you and what have you done with my friend?" Jason demanded, shaking Matt vigorously. Someone looking at the exchange would see a small, bespectacled boy shaking a boy that's all height and muscles, with the tall boy looking down at him as if he's considering how he'll taste for lunch.

"Are you done?" Matt asked drily.

"Yeah, I'm done. That was fun." Jason grinned and Matt flipped him off.

"Wow! Do you hold your mum with that hand?"

"Get away from here, man."

Matt turned towards the other direction, a small smile on his face as he headed towards his next class.

He hates school and nothing has been able to change that. It is quite ironic that his two best friends are two of the most intelligent people he knows and they thrive on school. As he headed towards woodwork class, perhaps the only class he can stand, his mind wandered back to Melissa.

What could have made her dye her hair pink? Almost everyone knows how vain Melissa is, especially about her hair. Since she heard her first blonde joke at 13, she had vowed to single handedly change the narrative about blondes and even when everyone was experimenting with their hair and changing its color, she maintained her natural blonde hair.

By the time Matt got to class, his mind was firmly in Melissa heaven and he couldn't get thoughts of a certain blonde's mane off his mind.

"It's going to be a long day." He murmured to himself.

Chapter Three

"Where is Melissa?" Jason asked, looking around suspiciously.

"She's not here yet. Are you going to stand there or you'll come over here?" Matt asked him.

Jason was standing by the entrance, in that safe little space between the main building and the roof. He ignored Matt and continued the conversation he had been having in his head where he had been trying to convince himself that it's not a bad idea to have lunch with his friends on the roof. What people didn't understand about him is that breaking rules wasn't his problem per se. His problem was convincing himself that it was a good idea to do so and that he stands to gain from it. Anything he can convince himself of, he can do. And at the moment, it was still hard to decide whether the odds of having fun outweighed the possibility of being suspended if caught.

"Just get over here. No one is going to catch us." Matt said, his grip on his patience apparently snapping.

"Hey, guys."

The sound of Melissa's voice from behind him made the choice for him and he stepped forward, flopping down next to Matt. He had a good view of their small town from where he was sitting and he decided that even if they were caught, seeing that view again was a good enough price to pay. They settled into a comfortable silence, the kind that is peculiar to people that have gone through the same motion several times.

"Why did they stop students from coming here anyway?" Melissa asked, breaking the silence. She had not exactly touched her food, just played around with it in her plate. That too was not entirely new, and Matt will probably end up eating it when he's done inhaling his own lunch.

"A student attempted suicide here last year, remember? And the parents demanded that they lock it." Matt responded with a mouth full of food. Melissa gave him a disapproving glare, but he just grinned at her and continued eating.

"I heard she wasn't trying to kill herself." Jason said, and then shrugged.

They settled into that comfortable silence again, both boys working hard at pretending that curiosity was not eating away the very core of their being.

"So, you're both wondering why I dyed my hair and why I came late this morning…" she began.

"We were? I wasn't. Jason, were you?" Matt said, humor dancing in his eyes and the three of them laughed. That was his thing. He was the group joker. A lot of people often wondered how the three of them are friends when they are so different from each other, especially Jason. According to the classifications in a regular high school setting, the three of them are from different levels of the social hierarchy. But somehow, they managed to defy all odds and stayed friends. Melissa often joked that one day, when she's rich and famous and she writes her first book, she'll dedicate a few chapters to talking about how to maintain friendships.

"That's if we are all still friends then." Jason had said glumly, and Matt and Melissa had thrown food at him and called him a party pooper.

"Ryan broke up with me." She said quietly, as if afraid that the wind would carry her words and carry it to unwanted ears. Eventually, everyone would find out anyway, they were already asking questions about her look. But she wanted to keep it away from the rest of the world for as long as it's possible to keep such things away from high school kids.

"Shit."

"What happened?"

The boys asked at the same time.

"You are not going to believe it." She breathed, "I don't even know where to begin."

"How about from the beginning?" Jason asked

Matt started at Melissa wordless and clueless. He had never seen her looking so helpless. She was the most fragile looking in the group with her delicate, elf-like features and certainly the most good looking. But she was the strongest member of their team, the glue that held them together and it was disconcerting to see her in such a weak and broken state.

"For a while now, things have been really bad between Ryan and I. Even before we went on summer break." She began.

"Define bad." Matt said. Something about her tone snagged at his attention and he sat up straighter.

Melissa eyed him carefully before she continued. "He was really struggling with his temper and he sometimes let it affect our relationship."

"Melissa, did he hit you?" Jason asked, his face turning purple.

"No. no. He didn't." she said quickly.

"What did he do then?" Matt asked tightly, seemingly struggling with his breathing.

"He got a little abusive, but not physically. He said some really mean stuff when he got that way. But he always apologized."

"Sure, that makes it all better." Matt murmured drily to himself, still struggling with his breathing.

"I found out that he had been cheating on me with a girl in his college for a while when he came back home for the break. We got into this very messy fight, words flew, fists flew and he broke up with me."

"So he did in fact hit you." Matt asked slowly to confirm.

Melissa looked away and a heavy silence descended on the group as the three of them struggled with their feelings. For Melissa, it was a feeling of extreme vulnerability she's not used to, even with her closest friends. She hadn't told her mother why he broke up with her, the poor woman would have had a cardiac arrest, and maybe gotten Ryan arrested. Matt and Jason on the other hand were dealing with an echoing in their head and going through a range of emotions all at once, the most obvious one being anger. Closely following that anger was guilt- how could they not have known?

"Melissa, why didn't you tell us?" Matt finally asked what the two boys were thinking.

"I couldn't bring myself to do that." She said, twiddling her thumbs and not looking at either of them.

"How do I admit that I was in one of those relationships where the guy treated me like crap even though I clearly deserved better? I used to advocate against that! Remember that rally that year? God, I almost got kicked out of school. The old timers were not pleased." She chuckled darkly and wiped the tears from her eyes before they could drop.

"Why did you stay?" Matt asked.

For the first time since she started telling them what happened, she met their gaze and held him.

"Because I loved him. It was crazy and stupid, but I loved that bastard so very much. I loved him so much that when he broke up with me, I wanted to be someone else so badly to hide away from my reality."

"Shit." Matt muttered, before following it with a string of colorful curse words all directed at Ryan.

"We are here for you, Mel. And you don't ever have to hide anything from us. We'll never judge you and we have your back. Don't we, Matt?"

"Always." Matt confirmed. He pulled Melissa into a hug and held her for a while before she hugged Jason.

"You know what?" Melissa said, forcing some cheer into her voice. "I don't need him. It's the final year of high school, then I get to leave this shitty town for college and I basically have my whole life ahead of me."

"That's the spirit." Matt chuckled and flicked her nose.

"Thank you, guys. For always."

"Stop it, please. We promised that we'll always have each other's backs and we'll always be there for the big things even if we miss the small things." Jason said.

When they got to high school, the strength of their friendship had been challenged because they had all grown into different people over the years and they had found varied interests outside their friendship. Melissa was one of the most popular girls in high school, and probably the most beautiful with her long legs, blonde hair, piercing blue eyes that always looked as if she knew something you didn't. If she hadn't been dating Ryan, all the boys would have lined up for a chance to be with her- not like they didn't, still.

Matt, who was also one of the cool kids, was on the school's basketball team and he was indispensable to the team. He was an occasional bully, but a really nice guy overall and he had an endless line of girls at his beck and call, even college girls. And then there is Jason, the nerd in the group. The skinny dude that gets knocked around quite a lot and only has Matt to thank that he was no longer being bullied. He was in the AV club, took all advanced classes and was at the bottom of the social ladder.

The three of them together in one group was the biggest social blunder one could make in high school, and it caused them to drift apart in their first year as high school students. But they learnt the hard way that they didn't have to follow the status quo, and they could in fact make their own rules, and so they did.

"Come on, little ones. Let's hug it out." Matt said, grinning affably at them. Both Jason and Melissa rolled their eyes, but they hugged him.

"No one says that group hugs are uncomfortable." Jason said, his voice muffled as he was pressed too tight to both of his friends.

"They make it seem like a fun thing in the movies." Melissa followed and Matt let go of them.

"You both disgust me." He eyed them, but there was a small grin on his lips.

"Come on, let's get out of here before we get busted." Matt stood up, brushed the debris off his pants and offered a hand to Melissa.

"How did you even open the gate?" Jason wondered.

"I picked the lock." Matt said proudly, winking at the both of them.

Jason shook his head at him and turned to Melissa as they headed back to the main building.

"Are you going to keep the hair?"

"Yeah, I think I just might."

"It suits you." Matt said grandly and winked at her.

"You really think so?"

"Yeah. You look like a hotter version of Harley Quinn. But without all the crazy."

"How do you know Harley Quinn?" Jason asked with a laugh. "I though you said you don't read my comic books."

"I make it a point of duty to know about hot girls, even the ones in comic books."

"Nerd."

"Oh, shut up."

They continued their friendly banter all the way to the school hall where they were getting strange looks from people, but Melissa didn't care. She was with her two best friends and maybe the last days of high school won't be so bad after all.

Chapter Four

The next few weeks were more trying than Melissa could have imagined. She discovered pretty quick that people could be nasty if they took it upon themselves to be. But as bad as it was, if she had known that what's to come will be even worse, she certainly would have found a way to enjoy it. But as far as she knew, her current reality is as bad as it could get.

"Where is Matt?" she asked Jason as she slid into their usual spot at their favourite restaurant in town. It was a Saturday and they had decided to have tacos together after a long week of barely doing anything together.

"He's late." Jason said, sipping his cola drink like it was liquid salvation.

"That's unusual." She muttered, looking around. The best part about coming here is that all the people they know don't come to eat here. Even in a small town, there are still places that are like stowaways. Few people know of its existence and the few that do know that they are indeed lucky because the food there tastes like it came from heaven's kitchen.

"He's been very busy with basketball practice. They have that big game."

"Oh, yeah." Melissa nodded. She had quit the cheerleading squad a week ago and she was trying to stay out of that scene as much as possible.

Fifteen minutes after Melissa arrived, Matt walked up to their table with a black eye, split lips and a big smile on his face.

"Jesus Christ!"

"Oh my goodness!" Melissa and Jason exclaimed, the both of them leaping up immediately and started asking him questions.

"What happened to you?"

"Were you in a fight?"

Matt stared at his friends as if they had suddenly lost their senses and he wasn't sure what they were looking alarmed for.

"Are you going to say something or you'll just stand there looking amused?" Melissa said, frustrated.

"Let's sit down, yeah? Believe it or not, but I am exhausted." Matt said drily and he lowered himself painfully on the seat. After a few seconds, Jason sat down and Melissa announced that she was going to get ice from the kitchen.

"What happened, man?" Jason peered closely at him, trying to gauge the amount of pressure that could have caused his eye to blacken like that.

"Nothing, just cold justice."

"What do you mean?"

They both turned in the direction Melissa had gone and understanding finally dawned on Jason.

"Please tell me you didn't do what I'm thinking you did."

"I wouldn't know what you're thinking, I'm not a smart ass like you."

"What does that..." Jason began then changed his mind. "Just tell me you didn't go and beat Ryan up."

"It depends, do you want me to lie to you?" Matt's eyes were shining with righteous indignation and it appeared that Jason was on his way there as well, except they both had different reasons.

"What? You could get arrested. What is wrong with you?" He demanded.

"Keep your voice down, will you? I don't want Melissa to know and I don't care about getting arrested."

"It could affect going to college!" Jason whined and Matt huffed dismissively.

"Piss on that."

"Matt..."

"No, stop. I don't get why you are so mad at this. That ass fucked our best friend over, our best friend.

You didn't think I was going to take that sitting down, did you? Or that I was going to buy into that pacifist bullshit Mel has been on. She might be over it, but I'm not."

"Isn't that just classic Matt." Jason said and laughed bitterly.

"What is that supposed to mean?" Matt demanded, his voice taking that cold, dangerous edge that most people knew better than to mess with. Jason apparently wasn't most people.

"You somehow made this about you, didn't you?"

"Are you implying that I'm self-centered?"

"I'm not implying it, I'm saying it. What if he comes for Melissa again out of anger at what you did? If you don't care about getting arrested or possibly even gang beaten by college boys, what of her?"

Matt stopped hearing what Jason was saying after he called him self-centered. All he heard was a static sound that went on and on and on. He stood up abruptly and Jason moved away in his seat, eyes frightened. Matt gave him a long, hard look and walked out of the restaurant without looking back.

"I'm back, where did Matt go?" Melissa asked Jason, her blue eyes scanning the room for him.

"He said he wasn't feeling too well and he had to go. He asked me to apologize for not waiting for you to return." Jason said calmly, smiling slightly at her.

"Oh." She said simply, disappointed.

Jason, noticing the disappointment took the ice bag from her hand and set it on the table.

"Hey, don't worry. We're still going to have fun. It's been so long it was just you and I hanging out, you know?"

"Yeah, I guess." She was still worried, but she smiled at Jason.

Jason was her oldest friend. Their mothers were friends so they used to have the same babysitter a number of times when their mothers went out together. They met Matt later and kind of took him in. It was more like he took them in because some of the bigger kids were picking on Jason in middle school and he made them go away. Even then, Jason had a smaller frame than other boys his age and he had to wear glasses as he was cross eyed then and that was being corrected. Ever since then, Matt went with them everywhere and they became a group.

"So, what's new with you?" she asked, humor dancing in her eyes. It was an inside joke Matt started based on the fact that Jason doesn't do well with new things. He liked order and change bothered him on a level that was almost obsessive-compulsive.

He rolled his eyes at her and sighed inwardly. Even when Matt was away, he still managed to hold sway. A strange feeling passed through Jason he didn't recognize, but Melissa was staring at him so he shoved it away to analyze later.

"You already know the answer to that." He muttered, then picked up the menu. He already knew what he would be having, but he needed something to do with his hands. Does he even know how to talk to her if Matt is not around?

Although he was at war with his emotions, none of it showed on his face.

"Oh, come on! No juicy gossip?" she teased and he gave her a long look.

"Yes, yes. I know. You are beyond that." She barely managed to get the words out before she burst into laughter.

He sat back and watched her laugh, a little smile playing on his lips. It felt good to be in the presence of a laughing Melissa again. She hardly laughed since the whole thing with Ryan started, it was like she was a different person. But now, it felt like just maybe the old Melissa isn't too far away from the surface.

"Hey, kids. What will you like to order?" Natasha, their favorite waitress asked.

"Natasha!" they chorused in a way of greeting and smiled warmly at her.

"Where is that one that flirts all the time?" she was referring to Matt, of course.

"He had to go take care of something at home." Jason responded.

"Oh, I'll miss him. So, what will you be having?" She brought out her small notebook. If Matt was around, he would have said something like, "Are you on the menu? Cos I sure won't mind having you."

"I'll have the usual." Jason said to override the silence left by the absence of Matt and his flirting.

"Of course you will, sweetie. I was asking Melissa." Natasha said, smiling sweetly at Jason.

"I'll have the chef's special." Melissa responded, laughing.

"Alrighty. That will take about twenty minutes."

She smiled at them again and turned away.

"Oh, come on. Why do you look so glum?"

"How do you just order the special? You don't even know if you'll like it"

"Oh well. I want to be surprised. If I don't like it, I'll eat out of yours."

"Of course you will." Jason smiled, wondering how it was just that simple for her.

"Have you started your college applications?" he asked to change the subject to something he could make good conversation at.

"Yes. I applied to California college of Arts and the Fashion institute of technology."

"That's so cool."

"I know, right? I'm quite nervous though. I keep wondering if I'm making a mistake and whether I should apply to a regular school and do something more marketable."

"First of all, fashion is marketable. Secondly, you should not doubt yourself, Mel. You are one of the smartest people I know and if this is what you want, I have no doubt you'll excel at it."

"My father thinks I'm wasting my big brains." She mumbled.

"He doesn't know anything; I think we can agree on that."

Their food arrived and they paused their conversation.

"This looks so yummy." Melissa groaned, taking in her meal. "Thank you, Natasha!"

"Bon appetite!"

"So, what about you? I have no doubt you're going for ivy league schools."

"I applied to MIT, CalTech and Princeton. They have excellent engineering programs and my chances of getting a scholarship is looking good."

"My baby is so smart!" Melissa said, reaching across to ruffle his hair and causing him to blush furiously.

"Stop it." He said, but with no bite to it.

"I can't wait for all of us to leave this shitty town and have lunch at expensive restaurants in classy cities." Melissa said dreamily and smiled broadly at Jason.

He debated telling her that Matt didn't intend to go to fancy colleges like them, but he let it be. Matt had not been in their conversation for a while and he was beginning to truly enjoy himself.

Chapter Five

Since the fight with Matt at the restaurant, Jason had been restless. Not because he had a fight with his best friend but because he suddenly found himself dealing with things he thought he had buried so deep they wouldn't find their way out. But there he was, struggling to deal with those things whilst trying to maintain his sanity.

He had not been able to study all weekend, and even playing the piano at the church didn't calm him like it used to before. He considered going over to Melissa's house, he knew she would love to see him. It had been so long he went to her house alone. Usually, they went to Matt's house during the weekends. Melissa took every opportunity to leave her father's expensive house, and he didn't mind being away from his fighting parents so they went to Matt's, the only one of them that has a normal family.

A bang on the front door brought him out of his mind's reeling. He ignored it, hoping it would go away if he just pretends not to hear it. But it didn't and he wasn't one to pretend a loud noise wasn't bothering him.

Reluctantly, he dragged himself downstairs, picking things up from the floor as he went. His parents must have gotten into another one of their throwing fights. These days, the sound of their fighting was the only loud sound he could successfully drown.

"Knocking the door like that won't make me open it faster. I'm coming!" he yelled at the person on the other side of the door.

"Jesus Christ, do you want to break…" he trailed off when he saw Matt standing outside, looking for all the world like someone killed his dog.

"Oh, hi." He grumbled, feeling guilty about how their last conversation ended.

"Can we talk?" Matt asked.

"Sure. Wanna come in?"

"Nope. I need to move." He was bouncing on the balls of his feet, full of nervous energy.

"Okay. Let me get my coat."

Jason locked the door behind him and they started walking.

"Your face looks better." Jason remarked without looking at Matt.

"My sister made it a point of duty to ice it and fuss all over me. It was agonizing."

"I'm sure it was."

They continued in strained silence for a while until Matt, not able to take it anymore broke the silence.

"What was that about?"

Jason sighs. He had been hoping to avoid having this conversation, or maybe even delay it for as long as possible.

"I don't know." He said simply. He did know, what he didn't know is how to explain why he acted that way.

"What do you mean by that? You called me self-centered when all I did was defend the honor of our friend. How was that me being self-centered?"

"It's just…I don't know how to say this without sounding like a jerk." He stopped walking and turned to look at Matt.

"It was just typical you, getting into fights and whatnot."

"Are you suggesting that it wasn't for a good reason? Because I seem to remember getting into fights because of you." Matt said, both arms crossed over his broad chest.

Jason sighed deeply, realizing how much of a jerk he was. He still couldn't bring himself to explain what happened to him, so he chose the shortcut to putting an end to this.

"I'm sorry, man. Really. I acted like a jerk and I apologize."

Matt gave him a long, hard look and although he still wanted to know why Jason snapped like that, he decided to let things go. Sometimes, peace was better.

"It's fine."

"Sure?"

"You know me; I don't hold things to heart for long."

"Thanks, bro."

They walked all the way to the park, talking about nothing in particular and stopping only to buy a hotdog. Or two, in Matt's case.

"I'm going to ask Melissa out." Matt announced when they were seated comfortably on one of the uncomfortable park benches.

Jason almost choked on the hotdog he was about to swallow. He took a deep breath and calmly chewed his food slowly, processing what Matt said all the while.

"What do you mean you are going to ask her out?" he asked when he finally swallowed his mouthful.

Matt shrugged. "What does asking a person out mean?"

Unable to hold himself, Jason snapped and some of that peace they had enjoyed on the walk went up in thin air.

"I just knew you were up to something when you decided to beat up her ex-boyfriend. That was your plan to get into her pants, wasn't it?"

"Hey, hey, easy champ." Matt said calmly, raising both hands in the universal sign of surrender. "I didn't say I want to get in her pants, I said I want to ask her out." He gave a fuming Jason a strange look, wondering what was eating him up so.

"What's your deal, man?" he finally asked, confusion and mild irritation chasing each other across the face.

"My deal is that you think you can get any girl you want just because you are you!" Jason yelled, causing a few people to turn their way.

"Okay, what is going on with you? You obviously have a problem with me, so start talking." Matt whispered furiously. It's a small town, it was only a matter of time before someone from school hears that they are fighting and spreads it through the gossip mill.

"I don't have a problem with you, I have a problem with you thinking you can just beat someone up and just like that win Melissa's heart."

"First of all, that's not why I beat Ryan, that loser had it coming for him the moment he started hurting her. Secondly, what's the big deal if I defended her honor because I want to get romantically inclined with her? I don't understand why you are so riled…"

Understanding dawned on him in that moment and he kicked himself mentally for not seeing it earlier. Of course, it all makes sense now- the outburst at the restaurant, his reaction now. How didn't he notice it?

"You are in love with her." He said. It wasn't a question and his expression dared him to deny it.

Jason opened his mouth and closed it a number of times, trying and failing to get any words out.

"Is that what this has been about?" Matt asked, running his hands through his hair.

"I have been in love with her since before I knew the meaning of love." Jason said quietly.

"Shit."

A heavy silence descended upon them again as they both battled with their thoughts.

"So what's it going to be?" Matt asked, completely at his wits end.

"I don't know. We let her decide?"

"No, that's not fair to her."

"All I know is that whatever happens, things will not be the same between us. Someone will get the girl; someone will be unhappy." Jason groaned into his palms.

"Except neither of us gets her. That's the only way I know peace can reign."

Jason removed his hands from his face and cut Matt a side glance.

"Do you mean that?"

"Yeah, sure. Shit. I can't believe I'm being the bigger person." Matt chuckled darkly.

"You're not being the bigger person. I have to give up on the girl I love."

"And you think I'm not in love with her? Or that this is any easier for me?"

"You get girls all the time." Jason said dismissively.

"Melissa isn't just any girl, and I should think you'd know that."

The pregnant silence descended on them again and they thought about simpler times.

"This is a mess." Matt said completely exasperated.

"You think?"

Chapter Six

Since he hit puberty, Matt had never had a problem with girls. He had never had one of those moments where he's sad and gloomy and the cause is a girl. Everyone knew him to be a flirt, and all his relationships have been more for the physical benefit than any kind of strong attraction. In fact, he didn't think himself capable of having such deep, romantic feelings. But Melissa has always been the exception and for the longest time, he couldn't bring himself to deal with his feelings for her. Instead, he flirted with any girl that let her gaze linger on him longer than was necessary and he distracted himself from what he felt for her. It was easier, given that she always had a boyfriend, so there was never really enough time to contemplate the what ifs.

But now, now there was actually a possibility that…he didn't let himself think that far. But for the first time in a long time she's single for longer than a week and he's suddenly not interested in any other girls.

A loud rap on his door brought him back to planet earth.

"Go away!" he yelled and began to shoot hoops with small basketballs.

"Matt, someone is here to see you." His dad yelled from outside.

"Great. Tell them to go away, I'm not home." He yelled back.

He heard his father talking to someone and he groaned, thinking it was one of the many girls on his list coming around to 'help him with his homework'.

The door opened and as he opened his mouth to make an excuse, he saw Melissa standing there like something he conjured from a dream. Her hair was in a high ponytail that showed off the elegant features of her face. Perfect heart shaped face, beautiful lips and the biggest, bluest eyes he had ever seen.

"Melissa, hi." He said, dropping the ball he was about to throw and rolling off the bed in his hurry to stand up. He landed with a thud and stood up immediately to face an amused looking Melissa.

"Did I interrupt something? Should I come back later?" She asked mischievously.

"Oh, come on in." he said, rolling his eyes. "What are you doing here?"

"You are not happy to see me?"

"Does such a thing even exist?" He rolled his eyes and stretched out his arms, "Come here, you."

He pulled her into a warm hug and it was only then that he realized he was shirtless. In fact, they both realized it at the same time and the hug got awkward.

"Erm, sorry about that." Matt said, trying to extract self from the hug but Melissa didn't let go.

"Mel?" he asked shakily, trying not to think of how close she is to him and how great her hair smells.

"Can we just stay like this for a bit? I could really use the hug."

Something about her voice broke his resistance and he melted into the hug.

"Are you okay?" he asked when the broke apart. He immediately went in search of a shirt while she made herself comfortable on his bed.

"Yeah, I'm just really exhausted. It's been a really long week; you know? What with exams and what not. Besides, I've been fighting with my father a lot." She said the last part with enough venom to make Matt know she's not sorry.

"What happened this time?"

"It's about my choice of college. He wants me to go to become some hotshot business person so that I can take over his company and I'd rather lose an arm."

"You could still study fashion and take over his business though." Matt opined.

"You are right, but I don't want to take over his business."

"You are his only child, what's going to happen when he retires?"

Matt sat at a healthy distance from her on the bed, ignoring the questioning raise of her brow at him.

"Are you taking his side?" she demanded.

"I'm not taking sides; I'm just being reasonable. Hear me out, okay?"

"Fine." She said defiantly; ready to shoot whatever he said down.

"Right now you are angry at your dad, and that is perfectly reasonable because he's not in support of your dreams."

"You are right about that." She grumbled.

"And like I said, you don't have to get any fancy business degree to know how to run the company. You can still pursue your dreams and have a say in how the company is run. You really don't want your family's legacy to go to waste because you are angry at your father now." Melissa regarded him for a while, turning his words over in her mind. She knew he was right and she desperately wanted to reject everything he said, but she knew he was right.

"Dammit. When did you get so smart?" She threw herself back on the bed and groaned, but not from the pain.

"I'm not all muscle, you know? Sometimes, I drop some really smart shit." Matt said, looking pleased.

"You don't say." Melissa said, eyeing him slowly. The atmosphere in the room changed- it suddenly became charged, so much so that they could feel it on their skin. A glint entered Melissa's provocative eyes as she eyes Matt seductively.

Matt has had his fair share of girls giving him the come hither look so he knew exactly what was about to happen and a part of him- a large part of him wanted it. But another part of him, the part that promised Jason he'd not make a move on her was screaming at him to get out. To get out now!

"Melissa…" he started, but that didn't stop her from crawling across the bed to him.

"Melissa…" he whispered again. This time, she was so close they were sharing the same breath.

"Yes, Matt?" she said slowly, running a finger down his left jaw.

Matt shivered and almost jumped up, but he was too weighed down by the weight of her lust filled eyes and seductive lips.

"Melissa." He said again, and gulped as she moved even closer.

"Matt. I'm going to kiss you now." She breathed against his lips and as much as he didn't want to, he wanted to even more. The thought didn't really make sense to him, but he lost the ability for rational reasoning the moment Melissa came so close he could smell the lavender on her skin.

Their lips touched and it felt like he was unraveling and being pieced together all at once. Like he was burning up and being doused by the greatest rainstorm ever. It was both painful and beautiful and he didn't want it to stop. He leaned in even closer and deepened the kiss, all the guilt he had been feeling completely silenced by the loud raging of his desires. It felt right, that moment felt right, like he had been born to kiss her and he wasn't going to apologize for it.

"I have wanted to do this for the longest time. God, you have no idea." He breathed into her hair.

"Is that so? What else have you always wanted to do?" she pushed, biting her lips.

"For one, I want to bite your lips. I can show you the rest if you're fine with it."

"Show me."

And he did, over and over until all of his guilt was washed away and replaced with the euphoric feeling of being with Melissa.

Chapter Seven

It took two weeks of Melissa and Matt hooking up for Jason to finally catch on to what was going on. Matt had told her that they should keep their relationship from people, including Jason, but he didn't tell her why. At least, not the whole story. If she's to find out about Jason's feeling for her, it wouldn't be from him.

Keeping their hands away from each other out in public was a real challenge and they slipped one day, and that's how Jason found out.

"The both of you are hooking up?" Jason demanded. They sprang apart immediately, but the damage had already been done. They were sitting by the bleachers after a basketball game. They had stayed back to make out, and it had landed them in trouble.

"Jason…" Matt began, but there really wasn't anything to say.

"Don't. I don't want to hear a word out of your lying mouth!" he was shivering with rage. He took several breaths to calm himself, but nothing was working.

Matt and Melissa took a few steps away from him; they had never seen Jason get mad.

"I didn't lie, man." Matt tried to explain.

"You didn't? And I'm guessing you weren't kissing her, you simply tripped and fell on her with your tongue going down her throat."

"Jason!" Melissa said, stepping between them. "What has come over you? So you saw us kissing, what is the big deal? In case you're wondering, I consented to the kiss for fucks sake." "Stay out of this, Melissa. This is between Matt and I."

"Who I kiss is between you and Matt? How dare you take that tone with me?" He sounded just as condescending as her father in that moment and she didn't think she would get that from one of her best friends.

"Easy, Melissa. He didn't mean it that way." Matt said, pulling her by the arm.

"Get your hands off me!" She cried and snatched her arm away from him. "Are you on his side now?"

"I am not taking sides. This is between Jason and I, you don't have to get involved."

She glared at him, but she didn't say anything more.

"Jason, I…" Matt began, turning to face Jason, but he didn't get to complete his statement and Jason hit him with a right hook right on the jaw.

"Jesus, are you made of steel?" Jason cried, cradling his hand. He flexed it a few times to see if his fingers are broken.

Matt took the punch standing, almost as if he didn't register the hit at all. The only indication that he was annoyed was the vein throbbing in his temple.

"Oh my God, Jason! What has come over you?" Melissa gasped, both hands covering her mouth, eyes wide in surprise.

"I'm going to give you a minute to apologize for that." Matt said, still regarding him with cold detachment, his eyes glazed over with anger.

"Or what?" Jason spat, still cradling his hand. "Or you're going to beat me up like you did Ryan?"

Matt's eyes went wide and Melissa gasped.

"You beat my ex-boyfriend up?"

"He deserved it."

"And you somehow thought it was within your rights to take justice into your hands?" she demanded.

"This isn't the time for this discussion, Melissa." Jason spat bitterly, "You can have it the next time you schedule an appointment to suck face."

Melissa gasped and took a few steps away from Jason.

"Don't talk to her that way, man." Matt said, "You can talk shit at me, but don't you ever take that tone with her."

"Okay, what is going on between the both of you?" Melissa demanded, staring back and forth between the both of them.

"Let's tell her, why don't we?" Matt said, grinning like a maniac.

"Matt…"

"Jason here is in love with you, Melissa. He has been since forever." Matt said without taking his eyes off Jason. He knew what he was doing, he saw it destroy him but he was beyond caring. He wanted to hurt him.

"How dare you?" Jason whispered, wheezing a bit.

"Oh my God." Melissa whispered, understanding dawning on her. It's true what they say that sometimes you think you want to know the truth about something, and sometimes you feel it too but as long as it's not directly in your face, you can pretend it is not there. Melissa might have guessed that Jason had a crush on her when they were younger, but she didn't give it a lot of thought, and she certainly didn't think he was in love with her…still.

"Well, that cat is out of the bag." Matt said, still grinning devilishly.

"Are you proud of yourself?" Jason demanded, looking for the entire world like he wanted to wring Matt's neck.

"Generally, yes, I am." Matt spat out.

"I can't take this. I'm leaving." Melissa announced and turned away without a backwards glance despite Matt calling out for her. Seeing Melissa leave like that finally made Matt lose the last grip he had on his temper.

"Are you happy now? She's gone. Jesus Christ." He ran a frustrated hand through his hair and kicked hard at one of the chairs.

"This is your fault." Jason spat and turned around to leave too.

Matt sat heavily on the exact spot he had been sitting while he was kissing Melissa a few minutes ago. That window of time was all it took apparently to lose some of the most important things in your life.

They have had several fights in the past, but this was different. They finally found the one thing that could truly tear them apart, and it's ironic that it's what brought them together in the first place- Melissa.

Matt and Jason didn't speak for a long time and Melissa didn't want to pick sides so she stayed away from them and they were all very miserable. Healing, they say, takes time and sometimes it's never truly complete. Sure enough, they started speaking again, but things were never going to be the same.

PART TWO

Chapter Eight

Melissa turned away from her desk to stare at the view outside her office. It is often said that when you see something every day, it becomes a part of you so much that you don't really see it. But the view outside her office still feels brand new every time she turns in her chair to look at it. Maybe it's because she makes it a point of duty to always look for something new out there, or maybe it's just too breathtaking to ever stop surprising her.

She had lobbied really hard to have her father's company moved to this building when they wanted to expand. It was one of the oldest buildings in the city, and probably one of the few things left in California that still has a soul, including the people. A lot of old buildings are being torn down to build the sky high monstrosities most people favored now, and in her opinion, they lack soul.

"What do you need a building to have soul for, Melissa?" Her father had asked her exasperatedly.

"Daddy, is this my decision to make or yours?" she retorted, not bothering to hide her irritation.

Over the years, she and her father had been able to build a relationship based on trust and mutual respect for each other. It had been hard to forgive him for years of neglect, but she did it for her mum and then for herself. A certain clarity comes with growing older and she has that to thank for their relationship.

"It's all yours, sweetie." He said and kissed her on the forehead.

So she had bought one of the older buildings and had it upgraded. It cost them a lot, but every time she looked outside her office and saw the ocean, she knew it was worth it a thousand times over.

The sound of her phone ringing brought her out of her reverie. The sun was just setting and the sky was an explosion of colors that reflected on the ocean, making both sky and ocean look like twin flames. It was for moments like that she wanted an office in this location. With a lot of difficulty, she turned around in her chair and picked up her phone. The name on the display warmed her heart even more than her office view. More than the sun.

"Hey, baby." His voice purred and her toes curled instinctively. Even after two years of being together, Rick's voice still had that effect on her. It was one of those things that always felt brand new.

"Hey, you." She replied, smiling with all her face. She couldn't help it; the man makes her unbelievably happy.

"Were you watching the sunset?" he teased.

"You know I was."

"And here I was, thinking about you. My poor heart."

"You certainly are not jealous of the sun now, are you?"

"I only have one sun, baby and every other thing pales in comparison to her."

There's a way he gave compliments that they don't sound like compliments. He makes them sound like hard facts, and if a person were to decide to make research on that matter, they would find it to be true. That's one of the other reasons she was hopelessly and completely in love with him. She has always been used to getting compliments and at some point, they all started sounding the same. But Rick made everything feel like something she has never heard.

"Stop it, Rick." She said, blushing furiously and giggling like a preschooler.

"It's date night tonight, what do you wanna do, baby?"

"I don't know. I've had a pretty long week. Can we just stay in today?"

"I've got you, baby. Chinese or pizza?"

"Pizza, please. With an overload of cheese."

"Anything for you. I'll pick you up around 5?"

"That works. I'll see you soon."

"I love you."

"I love you, too."

She was still blushing when she ended the call. Melissa had always been a privileged kid, and the fact that she's incredibly smart means not a lot of doors are closed to her. But, she has always been unlucky when it came to men. It got so bad that for a few years in college, she fancied herself a bi-sexual. That's how she met her best friend, Laura.

****

When she walked out of the office building at exactly 5 o'clock, Rick was waiting by his car. His unruly, dark hair was thoroughly tousled by the wind, but asides from that, everything else about him was impeccable. His Christian Dior suit that fit perfectly, silver Rolex she bought for his last birthday, and the man himself. He's the whole package, the kind that most girls can only dream about, the kind that she used to dream about. But here he was, outside her dreams and smiling at her like she's the best thing in his life.

He watched her as she walked towards him as if he was undressing her in his mind, and Melissa had no doubt that he was. Not that she minded at all.

"Damn. You are so beautiful, Melissa." He said soulfully when she was standing in front of him, and then he pulled her into a hug.

"Did you have a good day?" she asked him as he led her to the passenger's side.

"It's about to get better." He smiled at her as she got in, closing the door behind her.

They decided earlier on that they didn't want to be live together, not until they get married. So they spend the weekends together, alternating between his house and hers and it has worked for them so far.

"What was work like today?" she asked, stretching a little as her whole body started to relax at her proximity to him.

"Let's just say today reinforced by beliefs that humans are hard to deal with and I can't wait for the robots to come."

"And what makes you think the robots will be any better?" she chuckled.

"They are literally a walking, talking program; a program that can be edited to suit your needs. If they argue, it will be because I want them to argue with me. Otherwise, they will do exactly as I say."

"Controlling much?" she teased, but when he turned to look at her, his black eyes were hard and shining and she found it extremely arousing.

"I will show you controlling later tonight."

"Is that a threat?" she gulped.

"No, baby. Just a promise." He winked at her and turned his focus back on the road, leaving Melissa's thoughts to spiral wildly.

Chapter Nine

"Eleanor, pull up my schedule for tomorrow." Jason said to the virtual assistant he developed. Eleanor controls his smart house and all his devices.

"Hey, Jason. You sound stressed, you want me to play you something relaxing?"

"No, thank you Eleanor. Just the schedule is fine." There was a tiny bit of irritation in his voice, but he managed to reel it in.

"Okay. You have a meeting with your investors and board members' tomorrow by 9 am, you also have a business meeting at the country club by 3. Gym is for 5:30 and you are supposed to take your fiancée to dinner by 7."

"Shit. I completely forgot about dinner. I didn't make reservations!"

"Would you like me to make dinner reservations for you?" Eleanor asked.

"Yes, please." Eleanor is an advanced intelligent virtual assistant that he had developed to put on the market, but he ended up keeping her to himself mostly because she was a ground breaking piece of artificial intelligence and he wasn't ready to share her with the world. For the time being, he enjoyed being the only person that had a virtual assistant with such high level of sentience and functionalities.

"Do you have any preferences? Location? Menu?"

"Just pick somewhere that has a great view. Yolanda likes stuff like that." He said dismissively, and went back to working on his laptop while Eleanor searched for somewhere for him to take his fiancée for dinner."

"How about Daniel?" Eleanor suggested after a quick internet search. "It's a French restaurant, your wife should like that given the time she spent in

France. The food is also supposed to be so good you want to chew your tongue."

"And the ambience?"

"Magnifique." Eleanor said, switching to a flawless French accent.

"Perfect, make a booking."

"Done." She said after ten minutes. "I have put the details you'll need on your phone."

"Thank you, Eleanor. You make my life easy." He said in an offhand manner that suggested that he had said those words so many times.

"I aim to please, sir."

Jason smiled to himself as he continued to get more work done. He had indeed come really far for a kid from small town Oklahoma with little financial backing. The past few years have been kind to him, more than kind in fact and he had done better than he could have thought even in his wildest imagination.

He had started out as an engineering student in university, but one summer at Google changed his life. He went back to school, changed majors, and because he's incredibly talented, his scholarship wasn't discontinued. Immediately after graduation, he was employed as one of the software developers for Google, but he only stayed there for three months before he decided that he didn't want to have a boss.

The first software he built and sold was an amazing feat of technology that put America's wall street several years ahead of that of other countries' and put him on the 30 under 30 on Forbes list and since then, he has only been getting better and richer.

"Jason, just a friendly reminder that it's 5 o'clock, gym is in thirty minutes." Eleanor informed him.

He grumbled a quick 'thank you' but doesn't look up from his laptop, neither do his hands stop moving rapidly across the keyboard. After ten minutes, he finally looked up and heaved a sigh of relief.

"Can I lock your workstation now?" Eleanor asked.

"Yes, that will be all for today."

Another benefit of having Eleanor is that no one can hack into his system. Several hackers have launched a cyber-attack on him, trying to steal some of his work. In fact, the government tried to once, but not only did Eleanor ensure that the attacks were unsuccessful, she also traced them to their origin and fed him with the information. The more he thought about how completely perfect Eleanor is, the more he knew he never wants to share her with the world. It would probably make him the richest man in the world, but he would rather have something no one else has instead.

"Eleanor, now would be the time for that music." He said as he left his office. The sound of Beethoven's Piano Concerto No.5 accompanied him as he made his way to his home gym. He started working out the moment he knew he wanted to be famous, and he knew he wanted his name in magazines.

The Jason that left high school and the one that came out of college are two entirely different beings and sometimes, it felt to him like the part of him that existed before he went off to college never happened. The fact that he severed all ties with everything that connects him to that part of his life didn't help matters a lot. Yolanda only knew the part of him that started from college, the part he secretly calls "The New Jason".

It had caused a lot of fights between them, him not wanting to talk about where he came from, not even his parents. But they had reached a point of understanding that she's dating him, not his past or where he came from so it should not matter as such. It came up once in a while, but it never caused any real troubles anymore.

He worked out for one hour with the same laser focus he applied to his work and every other aspect of his life. His fiancée teases him that his focus could probably cut through diamond, and he'd just shrug and say,

"Probably." With a smug smile on his face.

His phone started ringing just as he was about to get into the shower.

"Answer call." He said to the house without moving to get his phone.

"Hi, Jason." A familiar yet strange voice filled the house, and for a few seconds, Jason stopped moving. In fact, his entire body went still as he tried to figure out whether what he heard was real or his mind was playing tricks with him.

"Jason, are you there?" the voice said nervously.

"I probably got the wrong number." the caller mumbled to himself then laughed shakily.

Jason could picture him at the phone-well, what he looked like ten years ago- so vividly it felt as if he was having an out of body experience.

"I'm here." His voice came out in a hoarse whisper.

"Hello, Matt."

"Hello, old friend." Matt said down the line, and he heard his grin down the line. Still shaken, he made his way to his bar. If he was going to make it through this conversation without being reduced to the boy he was ten years ago, he needed a stiff drink.

It's funny how a person tries to run from something and they change almost everything about themselves just to take them as far away from that thing as possible, but just a voice, a blast from the past can have them crashing back to that place. Jason was going to realize soon enough that you can only ignore some things, you can't completely escape them.

Matt let out a sigh of relief before he laughed long and hard.

"It's been so long, man. So damn long."

Ignoring the glass, Jason drank the vodka straight from the bottle. He contorted his face as the drink burned a path from his mouth, down his throat and into his stomach.

"Yeah, I would call seven years a long time too." He said mildly.

"You kind of went radio silence on us. After that last time, I just assumed you didn't want to stay in touch so I let it be." There was no reprimand in his voice, but Jason felt a tinge of guilt. Just a tiny tinge, and he killed it with another gulp of mouth burning vodka.

"Yeah, well. You assumed correctly, I guess." There was no point lying or making excuses for his actions. He had no regrets, and Matt knew that they stopped being real friends a long time ago.

"It's fine, really. I understand."

There was a moment of silence where Jason fumbled with what to say next. Eventually, he said,

"Is there a reason you called, Matt." He cringed when he heard himself, but there was no taking that back. Matt chuckled again, clearly not taking offence. Jason remembered that even then, it was difficult to rile Matt up.

"My old man died yesterday." he said, and even with the distance between them and the number of years of not keeping in touch, Jason could hear the poorly concealed grief and his heart broke for Matt.

Of the three of them, Matt was the only one that had a great relationship with his father then and the man was such a good man. The need to remove himself from his past didn't prevent him from being shaken by the news. Matt's father was one of the good things about his childhood, a consistent father figure when his own was drinking and smoking his life away.

"Oh God. I'm so sorry, man. I am truly sorry to hear that." Jason leaned heavily on the bar table. It had been such a long time since he was affected by a bad news like this.

"Yeah, thanks man."

"What happened?"

"He had a heart attack, and that was it. He didn't suffer and for that I'm glad."

"Is there anything I can do for you? Anything at all?" Jason heard himself say before he even fully processed the words in his mind.

"As a matter of fact, there is."

Chapter Ten

Melissa stretched languidly in bed, purring like a satisfied cat. Spending the weekend with Rick always had that effect on her. He knew exactly how to make her relax. She reached over to his side of his bed to touch him, but she only felt air. Curious, she opened her eyes and turned to his side of the bed, and she confirmed that he wasn't in fact in bed with her.

She laid in bed for a while longer, hoping he would return to bed, but when he didn't return after ten minutes, she stood up. Covering herself up in one of his shirts, she went in search of him.

The sounds of pans clashing directed her attention to the kitchen and she went in search of her lover, a small smile playing along the edges of her lips. Rick has always bragged about his cooking skill, but in all the time they had been together, he had never actually cooked.

"You're cooking." She observed, smiling. Her eyes lit up at the sight of him naked from the waist up, his sculptured chest barely covered by the apron tied around his waist and neck.

"That's a keen sense of observation you've got there, baby." He teased, not looking up from the soup he was stirring.

"Who do I have to thank for this?" she asked, her stomach rumbling at the truly delicious smell wafting up from the soup he was cooking.

"Hold on. Take a sit, I want you to taste this." He scooped some of the soup into a plate and offered it to her.

"What is this?" she asked, eyeing it skeptically.

"It's a chicken curry sauce; my mother's recipe."

"It smells good."

"Taste it."

He watched her very closely as she took scooped some up and waited for it to cool.

"Stop looking at me like that."

"I need to see the foodgasm play out across your face."

She rolled her eyes and took a sip of the sauce and immediately closed her eyes as an explosion of taste happened in her mouth. She closed her eyes to savor it, making small, moaning sounds as she chewed slowly.

"Oh my God, what is in this?" she asked when she finally swallowed.

"Like it?" he asked, crossing his hands over his chest.

"Love it." She ate what was left as fast as she could and handed the plate to him.

"Can I have more?"

"Not until you say that I'm a great cook, and you apologize for doubting my abilities."

"I'm sorry! Now, can I have more."

"Anything for you, baby. But first…" he pulled her out of her chair and held her close.

"Happy anniversary, baby." Her eyes went wide as she remembered. Of course! That's the special anniversary- It's their third year anniversary.

Lost for words, her eyes filled with tears and he pulled her into a long hug.

"I love you." She said fiercely.

"I love you too, baby. Come on, let me serve you. That was only the tip of the ice berg."

"I will never doubt your abilities ever again."

"Remember the last time you doubted I could do something?" he smiled slyly as her eyes went wide when she remembered.

"Oh my God." She blushed, and hid her face in her hands.

"I thought you'd remember." He winked at her and went to dish their food.

A few weeks after they met, he told her that he could make her cum five times in a row and she called his bluff on it. When they eventually had sex, it was so good that she ended up coming nine times in a row.

"Why have you never cooked when you cook this good?"

"Well, when we spend time here, we usually get too busy, if you know what I mean." He winked at her. "And your kitchen doesn't have more than what you'll need to make an omelet."

She tried to come up with an argument, but he was right so she just went back to eating.

"This is so delicious. I don't think I can get over it."

"I'll cook for you more often, I promise."

"I'll love that."

"I should probably make my kitchen more functional as well." She grumbled more to herself than to him, but he heard her.

"I don't think there will be a need for that." He said shyly, not looking her in the eyes.

"And why is that?"

"I was hoping, well…The thing is, we've been together for so long and I want us to take our relationship to the next level. I am totally and completely in love with you, babe and if you'll have me, I'd like to spend the rest of my life with you."

Melissa gasped, sitting back in her chair, not quite believing her ears. She had hoped this day would come, and here it was but all the waiting didn't prepare her. Nothing could have.

"Rick…"

He came to her side of the table, went down on one knee and brought out the most beautiful diamond and emerald ring she had ever seen.

"Melissa Theresa Browne, will you do me the honor of marrying me?'

"Yes. A thousand lifetimes of yes!" she responded, not bothering to hold the tears in anymore.

"I love you." He said as he slipped the ring on her finger.

"I love you too."

Melissa's phone started ringing from the living room while they kissed, and they ignored it. It continued ringing angrily until they stopped kissing.

"I should have turned that off." She hissed angrily.

"Just go get it, I'm not going anywhere."

"No. You are not."

She muttered all the way to the living room as she went in search of her still ringing phone.

"Hello?" she snapped into her phone without checking the caller ID.

95

"Easy, Tiger." An amused voice said, and she deflated a little as all the annoyance went out of her system.

"Matt?"

"One and only, Mels."

Chapter Eleven

"Wow. How are you, Matt?"

Melissa asked, not knowing what else to say. Receiving a call from Matt was the last thing she expected to happen to her, but then again, she didn't expect to be proposed to. So it was obviously a day for surprises.

"Oh, you know?" Matt said dismissively.

"Jesus, it has been how many years?" she said mostly to herself, suddenly feeling guilty.

"Too long, Mels. Too damn long." There was a twinge of sorrow in his voice and a new wave of guilt washed over her.

"I'm sorry, Matt." She said, sagging from the weight of the guilt.

"It's okay. I didn't reach out either."

"But you did, and I was a total bitch to you."

"It's fine. I got over that a long time ago. I actually called to tell you something." Something about his voice had her heart racing faster.

"Is everything alright?"

"I lost my dad, he had a heart attack."

Melissa gasped and sat heavily on the couch, tears already gathering in her eyes.

"I'm so sorry, Matt." She whispered.

"It's fine, he lived a happy life."

"Jesus Christ."

Matt let her sob silently for a while longer before he continued.

"I called to invite you to the funeral. I thought that you might like to pay your last respects to him."

"I would love to, Matt. Thank you for giving me the honors."

"It's no problem at all. I invited Jason too."

"He'll be coming?"

"If I'm to take his word for it, then yes."

"Looks like we'll be having that reunion after all." She chuckled darkly, recalling what happened right before they all left for college, and she knew they would not be staying in touch.

"Looks like it."

"When is the funeral?"

"Next Sunday. We'll be having a little family gathering on Saturday. I'll like for you to be there."

"I'll be there. How are you holding up? I know how close you both were."

"I dunno, Mels. It's almost as if I've not fully processed what happened. He was my biggest fan; you know? He believed in me when no one else did. I owe everything I am now to him and it's hard to believe that he's gone. So, I don't think about it, instead I just focus on the positive things."

"I can't even pretend to know what you are going through. Just hold it together, okay? And for what it's worth, I'm looking forward to seeing you. I wish it's under better circumstances, however." Melissa didn't even know how true those words are until she said them.

"I'm looking forward to it as well."

"Good bye, Matt. I'm truly sorry for your loss." Melissa turned around to find Rick staring at her. She didn't know when he came in, she had been that engrossed in the conversation with Matt.

"Problem?"

"A blast from the past."

His forehead crinkled in confusion. They talked about everything, so he knew a lot about her past relationships, and both past and present friendships.

"What part of it, exactly?"

"That was Matt."

"Oh." He knew Matt, of course, and all that had transpired between them.

"He lost his father, he asked invited me to the funeral next week Sunday."

"Oh, shit. I'm sorry about that."

"God, I loved that man. You know how every group has a dad and a mum? Matt's parents were the group's parents. Matt's dad used to drive us to playdates, to the park, ice cream place, just name it. If anyone of us had a show or a game, he was there. Jason's father was deadbeat, but Matt's father went to every one of his science shows and cheered louder than anyone else in the room. I remember that one spelling bee I had really been hoping my dad would show up to." She laughed bitterly, "He didn't attend, of course, but Matt's dad was there. I don't think I would have been able to keep my shit together if he wasn't there. He took us as his own and showed up for each of us, both together and individually. When we stopped really being friends, it really broke his heart. Jesus, I feel so terrible."

Melissa turned to Rick and cried as if she had lost her own father. In a way, it felt like it because the man had been there for her while her own father was still trying to decide what was more important in his life.

"I'm sorry, baby. Is there anything you need me to do? You know I've got you."

"Will you come with me to the funeral? I know it's a lot to ask, but I'll really like to have you there. I've not been back home in a long ass time and I don't know if I'll handle going back home well."

"It's not too much to ask. Of course I'll come with you."

"Thank you!" she held on to him harder and placed her head on his chest, feeling safe and entirely at peace. Well, almost at peace.

"Melissa?"

"Yes, baby?"

"Let's get married."

"You did just give me that beautiful ring. Of course we'll get married."

"No. I mean, let's get married soon. We could go to the court house and make it legal. The celebration and all that can come later."

"Really?" she looked up at him.

"Yes. I love you so much it hurts and all this talk about loss…" he trailed off, took a deep breath and continued.

"I don't want to waste any more time. I want to spend every bit we have legally bound to you, heart and soul."

"Okay." Her eyes were shining as she nodded vigorously.

"Okay?"

"Let's get married."

"Yes!" he whooped and spun her around.

"I am the luckiest man alive. Believe that."

"And I'm the luckiest girl alive."

****

"Hey, you."

"Sup sweet cheeks?" Laura said down the line, sounding as if she had food in her mouth. Melissa had no doubt that she did. Laura was one of those girls other girls hated because they could eat anything and not get fat. The worst part is that she is a chef in one of the best restaurants in town.

"What are you eating?" Melissa asked, just out of curiosity.

"I am so glad you asked. I stole this cake from work and you absolutely have to taste it. It tastes like sin, Mels. I could go to hell just for this cake."

Melissa giggled. Of course she would say something like that about food.

"You are going to hell, anyway."

"Shut up." Laura said and they both laughed.

"I have news." Melissa announced, eyeing her ring and smiling to herself.

"Hmmm. Hit me." Laura said with her mouth stuffed, her words coming out muffled.

"Rick asked me to marry him." She squealed. The original plan had been to go over to Laura's and break the news to her, but she didn't have a lot of time on her hands and things would be moving faster than she could have ever dreamed. Hell, she'd be getting married to the man of her dreams in two days!

"Oh. My. God!" Laura screamed down the line and Melissa had to remove the phone from her ear. Anticipating more shouting, she placed the call on loudspeaker.

"Tell me everything! Why isn't this call a Skype call? Girl, I want to see the ring!"

"Of course you do." Melissa giggled, wondering how she met such a drama queen.

"Now, Melissa. Skype!"

"Okay. Okay."

It took all of ten minutes to find her laptop and connect to Skype. When Laura's face appeared on the screen, she had the funniest expression on her face.

"Girl, why are you laughing? Show me the ring!"

Melissa put her hand up to show Laura the ring, enjoying her 'ohh-ing' and 'ahh-ing' sounds.

"That ring is fucking beautiful. I'm so happy for you." Laura sniffed and Melissa burst into laughter.

"Are you crying?"

"Shut up. My lash is stuck in my eye, is all." She sniffed again and Melissa continued laughing.

Laura isn't one of those people to show their emotions in this manner. She would rather use humor and sarcasm to express how she feels. But to see her crying…that's something that hardly ever happens.

"I'm so happy for you. I can't think of anyone that deserves this more." She sniffed again, dabbing furiously at her tears.

"Now you're going to make me cry."

"I'm sorry. Fucking hormones."

They both laughed and cooed at the ring some more.

"There is one more thing."

"Oh?"

"I have to go back home by Friday and Rick is coming with me. Rick and I have decided to get our marriage legalized before we have to go."

"This Friday?" she asked, a stupefied expression spelling itself across her face.

"Yes. We'll be going to the court on Thursday and I was hoping you'd come with me."

"Wait. Are you pregnant?"

"What? No!" Melissa cried incredulously. "I'm not pregnant!"

"What's with the rush then?"

"I love him, Laura. And he loves me. We want to be together. It took us long enough to arrive at this point and we don't want to waste any more time. When we return from Oklahoma, we'll make plans for a wedding party and all that."

"That's so beautiful. Of course I'll come with you to the court house, you didn't have to ask."

"Thank you." Melissa breathed a sigh of relief inwardly, glad that Laura understood.

"Why are you going to Oklahoma, anyway? Didn't you hate it there?" Laura continued her assault on a piece of cake that looked truly moist and delicious.

"It had its good parts. It wasn't all bad."

"Interesting. Your mood turned dark every time I brought it up so I assumed you completely hated it there."

"No, not completely. I only started hating it there towards the end of high school." Melissa said wistfully.

"So why are you returning? It sounds urgent."

"Someone died. I…I really don't want to get into the details right now. We just shared a happy moment, I don't want to ruin that."

"It's okay, baby. You can always tell me whenever you are ready."

"Oh my god, you're getting married! You are actually getting married!"

"I know! I feel like I'll wake up tomorrow and still not believe that I'm engaged." Melissa beamed at her friend, going with the flow. Laura always knew how to distract her from whatever was hurting her, and whenever she was ready to talk, she would always be her safe space.

Before she met Laura, she never had any serious female friends. But the tiny blonde walked into her life like it was her God given right and she made herself feel right at home, and to Melissa's surprise, she found that she didn't mind at all.

"Is it too early to start talking dresses? Cake? Venue? Do you have anything in mind at all? There is so much to be done!"

"Oh God. You're going to take over everything, won't you?" Melissa sighed good naturedly.

"As opposed to what? Leaving you to do it? We both know how nonchalant you can get sometimes and I refuse to allow you half ass your wedding!"

"But…"

"No buts, Melissa. This wedding will be covered in magazines, we go hard or we don't go at all."

"It's a wedding, not a basketball game."

Laura cut her a long, hard glare and she raised her hands in surrender.

"I have a dress in mind." She said dreamily, thinking back to the time she first entered an Alexandra Wang showroom and thought she was in heaven.

"That's more like it! Who do you want to wear?"

"Alexandra Wang."

"That's my girl."

"We should meet for coffee tomorrow, yeah?"

"Okay."

"When do you think you'll be returning?"

"I'm not sure, but we don't intend to stay beyond the weekend."

Chapter Twelve

Matt watched the rain from the window in his study, whiskey in hand. The day had started out clear, no rain clouds in sight and all of a sudden, the clouds turned dark and angry and the downpour started. It had been raining for two hours straight and he was getting worried. Both Melissa and Jason would be flying into town, and although they declined his offer to come pick them up at the airport, he was still worried about them.

"What time are your friends supposed at arrive?" Beth, his younger sister asked from behind him.

"They should be here by now." He murmured without turning away from the window.

"I'm sure they are fine." She moved closer to him and laid a comforting hand on his shoulder.

"I hope so." He clenched and unclenched his free hand.

After his father's death, he had been just a little paranoid, especially with the people he cares about. So when the phones started ringing, he rushed over immediately to pick it.

"Hey, Matt. It's Melissa."

A wave of relief washed over him and he sighed deeply.

"Hi, Mels. Did you arrive safely? I've been so worried."

"Yes, we did. Thank you. We are at the hotel now. What's with this rain though? There was no rain in the weather forecast yesterday."

"We are just as surprised." Something about what she said snatched at the edge of his memory.

"Did you say we?"

"Oh, yeah. I came with my husband."

"You are married?" he blurted out before he could think about his reaction to the news.

"Yes! I'll tell you all about it tomorrow."

"Okay. See you tomorrow. And, Melissa…welcome home."

He ended the call and turned around slowly to face his waiting sister.

"I take it Melissa is in town then."

"Yeah." He downed the rest of his whiskey in one smooth gulp and spread his hands.

"Looks like that reunion is actually going to happen." He smiled bitterly at her and she sighed.

"Are you okay?"

"I'll be. Come on, go back to what you were doing. I'm good here."

He turned went back to continue watching the downpour, drowning out his thoughts with the sound of the rain hitting the ground. The news of Melissa's marriage hit him harder than he could have thought possible. They all moved on years ago and they had not exactly stayed in touch. It was only natural that she met someone else, and she apparently did. And married him too. He didn't want to dwell on why he was shaken by the announcement.

I wasn't expecting it is all, there is nothing to it.

He said to himself, but even as he tried to convince himself of that, he knew it wasn't completely true. The phone rang again and he hurried to answer it, hoping it was Jason. Talk about 'saved by the bell.'

"Matt?"

"Hey, Jason. What's up, man?"

"Our flight got delayed. There is apparently a heavy rain falling over there and the visibility is poor."

"Oh, shit. Yeah. I was hoping you'd beat that."

"Unfortunately, I didn't. I'll probably be arriving later tonight or tomorrow morning. I'll keep you posted."

"Alright. Stay safe out there."

"I plan to."

Matt felt better knowing both of them were safe for the time being. He went downstairs to inform his sister and continue to make plans for the get together the next day.

"Jason is still out in New York; he'll fly in later tonight or tomorrow morning."

"The rain?"

"Yup."

Beth was catering the event, and although she had people to help her, she insisted on doing some things by herself. Matt had no doubt it was a way to work through her loss. He needed to do something to keep his mind occupied so he rolled up his sleeves and asked to help.

She eyed him suspiciously.

"You want to help me?"

"Well, yeah. You look like you could use some help." He gestured vaguely at her work table.

"I don't." she deadpanned, still eyeing him suspiciously.

It was true; everything looked to be under control. When it comes to her work, Beth has some undiagnosed case of serious OCD. He often wondered why she didn't carry that same attitude into other aspects of her life. It was probably for the best, she'd be a complete witch if she sought this same amount of control outside her work.

"I have everything under control." The oven timer went off and she brushed past him to remove a batch of delicious-smelling chocolate chip cookies, their father's favorite. Matt stared at it for a long time as nostalgia hit him and a memory of their father stealing cookies to hide in his stash in the basement crossed his mind.

Beth was saying something, but he didn't hear her, not until she waved her hand right in front of his face.

"Can you knead dough?" she asked and he could see the sympathy in her eyes.

"Why do you think these arms are strong?" he winked at her and took over the kneading from her.

"Take a break, you could use it."

She sighed and flopped heavily on one of the kitchen seats.

"I miss him so much." She said into her hands. The words were muffled, but he heard her nonetheless.

"You and me both, sis. You and me both. I still can't believe he's gone."

She sighed deeply and shook her head vigorously as if she was shaking off some memories.

"So, your old friends, huh?"

"Yup. I still don't know how that will go."

"You are all grown now. Surely, you can't let an incident that happened ten years ago still hang between you guys like a bad cloud."

"You would think so, but that bad cloud has stopped us from staying in touch over the years even though we knew where to look if we wanted to."

"Why didn't you?"

"I dunno. After high school, it seemed everyone wanted to escape or something."

"It's cute how you're defending them and making it seems like none of you tried to reach out to the others. You didn't try to escape from anything and dad told me you tried to reach out to them a number of times." She said scathingly.

"He insisted." Matt shrugged and went harder at the dough than he probably should have.

"I still don't understand. You guys were the friendship goal. I remember how I used to wish I had the kind of friendship you guys had. I used to dream about it!"

"Everything comes to an end, I guess. Even good things, especially good things."

"Do you think you'll all be able to settle whatever the problem is?"

"I guess we'll find out."

Chapter Thirteen

Driving into Matt's childhood home felt very much like going back in time as everything looked exactly as she remembered it from all those years ago. The swings were still out front, the plats that were Matt's father's pride and joy, the porch that looked like something from a different time even then- everything was exactly as she remembered.

"Are you okay? You seem distracted." Her husband, Rick said. Referring to Rick as her husband still made her feel tingly all over.

"It feels like someone paused time and gave me access to the past. This is exactly how this place looked like ten years ago. So many memories attached to this house- it felt more like home to me than my own home."

"The house you grew up in is way better than this." Rick said dismissively and it rubbed her off the wrong way. She immediately felt the need to defend this place.

"It's not the size of the house or how expensive it is that matters, but how safe you feel in it. I felt safer and more at home here than in my own house."

"I see."

There was that tone again and Melissa didn't like it one bit.

"What is it?"

He looked at her and sighed. "It's just…we're going to the house of one of your high school lovers and you probably made love here. I can't possibly share your sentiments, Melissa."

She turned to him, understanding dawned on her as she realized what was going on.

"Wait, are you jealous?"

"No." His eyes as he turned to look at the house said something else however. Melissa burst into a fit of laughter.

"Yes, you are! That is so cute! You have nothing to worry about, come on."

"Whatever." A small smile played at the edge of his lips and Melissa knew that all was well again.

"Come on, they must have seen us pull up into the drive."

"Are you nervous?" Rick asked as they walked towards the house.

"A little. What if I don't recognize them? Or what if they don't recognize me?"

"Now you just sound crazy." Rick said, and he threw his head back and laughed.

The door flew open before she raised her hand to knock.

"Hey, Mels." Matt stood there, as handsome as he was in high school. Maybe even more handsome.

"Hey." They stood there, staring at each other for a while before Matt pulled her into a hug.

"It's nice to see you again." He said warmly, and as she looked into his sea green eyes, she felt all that nervousness wash away from her body. It appeared that Matt still had that same calming effect on her.

"Nice to see you again too, Matt. Meet my husband, Rick. Rick, Matt."

Both men shook hands politely.

"Sorry for your loss." Rick said and handed the wine he brought from home over to him.

"Thank you." He looked at the wine and nodded in approval.

"You know your wines. Melissa, he's a keeper."

And just like that, the small tension eased away and Matt invited them inside.

"Is, erm, Jason here?" She had held back from asking about him the last time she spoke with Matt deliberately. For some reason, she knew it would not be as easy with him as it is with Matt.

"No, not yet. His flight got delayed yesterday because of the rain. He should arrive in the next hour or so."

The living room was filled with quite a good number of familiar faces, Beth, Matt's sister being one of them. She left Matt and Rick together to go say hi to Beth and the other faces she recognized.

By the time a knock sounded on the door, Melissa was already beginning to feel slightly at home, but she tensed up immediately she caught Matt's expression.

Matt returned a few minutes later with a stylishly dressed young man that looked nothing like Jason. But when his eyes caught hers across the room, she knew that it was in fact Jason.

Woah.

He smiled at her, but there was no hint of the shy boy he used to be. Melissa wore her confident business smile and crossed the room to say hello to her former best friend after almost ten years.

"Hello, Jason."

"Melissa." Jason took her hand in his and planted a kiss on it, taking her aback completely. She has had years of practice of hiding her surprise, so she smiled right back at him as if she was used to this happening.

Matt made a sound that sounded like he was in pain.

"Come on, we should begin soon."

Melissa introduced Jason and Rick, and it turned out they had met at a conference once.

"Family and friends, thank you for honoring my late father with your presence. My sister and I are really grateful that you decided to come celebrate our father's memory with us. You know, when I think about the parts of my father's life that I witnessed, I think I only ever saw him sad once, and that was the day my mum died. And even then, he found a way to comfort us and give us something to cling on to. He said, "Don't cry, champ. Your mother is in a place without pain, and you can bet that she has her legs up, drinking the finest wine and ordering everyone around.""

Everyone laughed, and soon enough, they were all sharing some of their fondest memories of Matt's father. The three friends found themselves laughing over shared memories, memories they had forgotten all about till now.

"Remember when your dad gave us the talk?" Jason said, and Matt groaned.

"What? I don't know that story." Melissa said immediately, looking from Jason to Matt, eyes narrowed.

All the other guests had left and Rick had excused himself, to give Melissa some space to reconnect with her friends. The three of them were sitting by the fire in the study, drinking the wine Rick had bought and trading the more scandalous stories they couldn't share with the other guests.

"There is a reason why you don't know it." Matt deadpanned and Jason burst into a drunken laughter.

"Come on, I wanna know!"

"You brought it up, Jason. Tell the lady the story."

They both turned to Jason expectantly.

"Fine! Okay, so I crashed at Matt's overnight because my parents were having another one of their big fights and I didn't want to stay with them. I lied that Matt had a sleepover and I had to be there, so they let me go."

"Sleepover? How old were we then?" Melissa interrupted and both Matt and Jason gave her a scathing look.

"Do you want to hear the story or you want to keep interrupting?"

"What? I just want more information. That's all." She whined and Matt gave in.

"We were 13." He looked at Jason for confirmation, and he got it.

"Please continue." Melissa said primly, turning to Jason.

"He found one of Matt's Playboy magazines, and he thought we were old enough to get the talk. It has to be one of the most embarrassing moments of my life if I'm being truthful."

"Oh God. He was trying to be cool about it, but somehow he still managed to weird everyone out, including himself. It was painful to watch and to live through." Matt groaned and Melissa laughed at the both of them.

"Remember how he was trying to teach us to use condoms to make sure we're protected?" Jason asked Matt, looking like he was slightly in pain himself.

"Jesus, please don't remind me."

Melissa doubled over in laughter and both men continued to stare hard at her.

"Why are you laughing so hard? Don't you have any embarrassing stories that involved my dad?" Matt demanded.

"Seems highly unlikely. It was almost as if the man made it his life mission to embarrass us."

"I think it was." Matt confirmed and he clinked glasses with Jason.

Jason excused himself to receive the call that came through while Matt continued to prod Melissa for a story and she continued to deny the existence of any story.

"I have to go." Jason announced glumly when he returned, his expression resembled the dark clouds that were beginning to form outside.

Chapter Fourteen

"Did something happen?" Melissa asked carefully. They might have spent the past few hours bonding over shared memories, but it was no evidence that things were smooth between them again.

"Apparently, my fiancée thought it a good idea to fly down here even after we already discussed it and I asked her not to."

"You're engaged?" Melissa asked, her jaw dropping.

For a few seconds, Jason looked part confused and part irritated, but then he remembered that on several levels, these people are still strangers to him, and he to them. The look cleared from his face and he offered an explanation.

"I got engaged a year ago, her name is Yolanda."

"And you didn't want her to come down here with you?"

"No, I didn't. I…" he looked at the both of them, both friends and strangers at the same time and decided that maybe it was time he let go of some of the barrier he had intentionally placed between him and them. Ten years is a long time to hold a grudge.

"I needed the space, I guess. Things have not exactly been going great between us." He admitted, not meeting either of them in the eyes.

"And she's here." Matt whistled.

"Yup."

"So what are you going to do? Can you persuade her that you need the space and convince her to go back to New York?" Melissa asked.

"I guess we'll find out."

He turned to Matt.

"Once again, I'm sorry for your loss. I'll see you at the funeral tomorrow."

He shook hands with Matt and hugged Melissa briefly before he turned around to leave, muttering cusses at no one in particular under his breath.

"Do you want to be on your way too?" Matt asked Melissa, biting his tongue a bit when he heard how hopeful he sounded.

"No, I'll help you clear up."

"You don't have to do that."

"I know, but I want to."

They move around the room silently, picking up plates and wine glasses and heading to the kitchen with them.

"Do you still live here?" she asked, doing her best to keep her voice as light as possible.

"No. I have my own place. It's so far from town it almost doesn't count as being in town." Melissa laughed at the picture he created.

"Is there a reason why you got a place so far away?"

"You know how it is here. Everyone is in everyone's business. I don't want anyone in my business."

"Good enough." She agreed. "So what do you do around here? For work I mean."

He stopped what he was doing and turned to face her fully, an amused expression on his face.

"I'm sorry if I'm being intrusive." She said immediately and turned away.

"No, of course not. It's just funny how we used to be able to talk about anything and everything without this lingering awkwardness. I know that it's been a while..." Melissa chuckled at that and he smiled knowingly.

He continued, "It's been a while, but let's pretend those years of separation don't exist. Is that something you can do?"

"I can try." She beamed at him and Matt's heart raced just a bit faster.

"I run a construction company from out here. We get contracts from all over the states, so I travel a lot. I don't have to, but I enjoy doing it."

"That's really awesome, Matt. I'm proud of you."

"Thank you."

"I see that you took my advice." He said after a while. He was doing the dishes while she dried them.

"Which?"

"Your father's company."

"Oh, yeah. That. It's the best advice I've ever gotten. I run my father's company and I also have my fashion business. It's a lot to juggle but I love every bit of it."

"I'm glad."

They continued their chore in silence, but not the strained type.

What sounded very much like rocks hitting the roof broke the silence and the both stared at each other, perplexed.

"Looks like the rain has picked up again."

"That's not rain! It sounds like we're in the middle of a natural disaster." She cried running to the closest window to see how heavy the rain really was.

"Looks like someone has been living in Los Angeles for too long." Matt mocked her, joining her at the window.

"This is insane." She muttered.

"It's no biggie. It will stop falling in a few hours at most and I can drive you back home."

"Alright, thank you."

"Damn, that's some heavy rain." Matt whistled, still looking outside. It was only 5 pm and everything had darkened so much that it looked like 9 pm.

"More like a storm."

A bolt of lightning flashed across the sky at that moment, suddenly lighting the world up, and as if annoyed by the bright light, deafening thunder followed immediately after. A strong wind shook the house and both Matt and Melissa exchanged a look.

"You might be right about that storm. Come on, help me bolt all the windows and let's go get another fire going."

Melissa shivered a bit at the mention of fire- It had suddenly gotten very cold in the house.

She bolted the windows while Matt went to get a fire going. By the time she was done, it was considerably warmer in the house.

"You still drink your coffee the same way" Matt asked when she entered the kitchen.

"Yes, please." She said, curious to see if he actually remembers how she liked her coffee.

She took a tentative sip and smiled into her mug when the ridiculously sweet and creamy taste hit her taste buds.

"You remember." She said simply.

"Of course I do."

"How do you do it, Matt?"

"Do what?" He peered curiously at her from the top of his mug.

"Even when I wasn't so receptive of you, you still tried to reach out to me, until you eventually stopped. I have no doubt you did the same with Jason. And today, you were just…I don't know, really. It was almost as if nothing happened between us and we were just having another one of our hangouts."

Matt set his mug down gently and fixed her with a look so intense she took a step back.

"You know; the fact that I don't have you guys like I used to hurt me every single day for the past ten years. Every day, I'd think about what I could have done better. I'd think that if I had just held back, maybe we'd all be great friends still. So I made it a point of duty to try, until I can't try anymore. I'm just trying, Mels. After high school, I realized just how crazy the world out there is. There are different kinds of people and not a lot of them give two fucks about you, even the ones you'd think will have your back disappoint. Having people that understand you and accept you for who you are is rather hard to find, so you can imagine that I missed what we had. I still do."

Melissa didn't know what to say. Was she supposed to apologize? She felt like she needed to, especially since she blamed herself for what happened between them, not like she ever admitted it like the way Matt just did.

"You are a better person that I am, Matt." She said quietly, her voice almost coming out like a whisper.

"What do you mean?"

"I wanted nothing more than to be rid of this place and everything in it. When my parents moved to California, it was the perfect excuse to never have to return. You guys meant the world to me, yet it was so easy to let all that go. You are the best of us and I am truly sorry I have been a shitty person."

"Apology accepted." He smiled at her, the kind of smile that came from deep within the soul and is reflected in the eyes, and Melissa relaxed a bit. She didn't know how tense she was until he said those words.

"Thank you." He winked at her.

The shrill sound of the house phone stopped her from saying any other thing.

"I'll get that."

Matt left her to her thoughts and returned later with the phone.

"Rick wants to speak with you." His lips were pressed into a thin line and Melissa wondered what that was about as she took the phone from him.

"Hey baby."

"I've been trying your cellphone, you got me worried." Rick responded, his voice sounding as if he was talking to her from the bottom of the ocean.

"I'm so sorry, my phone must have died. The rain caught me at Matt's. He'll drive me to the hotel once it stops."

"I don't think that will happen soon. The weather forecast predicts this will continue for the next six hours thereabout." He sounded tensed so she rushed to reassure him of her safety.

"It's alright, Rick. I'm safe here."

"Yeah, okay."

He still didn't sound convinced, but there wasn't much she could do.

"I'll check in every hour. How about that?"

"Okay. That could work. And once it is safe to move again, I'm coming to get you myself."

"There really isn't any need for that. Even after it stops raining, it might still not be safe to drive on these roads. Matt has a truck; it is safer on the road than the rental."

"Okay, baby. Take care of yourself."

"Problem?" Matt said from behind her when she got off the phone. She shook her head and handed him the phone, then she remembered his expression earlier.

"Matt, what was that face about?"

"What face?"

"When you handed me the phone, you looked like…I don't know, you had a displeased look on your face."

"Oh? I didn't realize it."

His mouth said the words but his face said something else entirely.

"Matt…?"

"Okay, fine. I don't like the guy."

"It's not your place to like him." She said tightly.

"I know, and that's why I've been trying to be polite, but something about him has been pulling at something in my memory and for the life of me I can't remember what that is."

"Do you know him?"

"No, I don't think so."

"Then tell your memory to behave.' She snapped.

"I'm sorry, Mels."

"She crossed her arms over her chest and doesn't say anything.

"Come on, Mels. I'll behave, I promise. I don't want to lose you again."

He pulled her into a hug and she eventually relaxes against him. The hug extends longer than either of them planned.

"Thank you." Melissa said, stepping away from his hug and feeling extremely guilty.

"Anytime." His voice had gotten deeper, somewhat.

"Do you think Jason would have settled with his fiancée?"

"I guess we'll find out tomorrow."

Chapter Fifteen

The storm eventually subsided around 3am, and by 5am, Matt was driving Melissa to her hotel. They had fallen asleep rather early, and when she tried his cellphone and the hotel phone when she woke up, he didn't pick up.

"Hey, don't worry. He probably just overslept too." Matt said to her, trying to assuage her fears, but it didn't work. She continued looking out the window at all the passing cars.

"He's really stubborn and protective of me. When I didn't call and neither of us picked the phone, he might have taken it upon himself to come looking for me."

Matt didn't say anything again after that, instead, he sank into his thoughts. He had promised her that he'd behave, but there was still something about the man that rubbed her off wrongly, especially after she told him about their court marriage.

You're just jealous. His inner voice said, but he actively ignored it. He didn't think it was jealousy. Granted, he always had a bad feeling about all her boyfriends, even then, but this was different. In his line of work, he has had to deal with different types of people- the honest ones, the ones that will rob you blind if they find a weak spot, the ones that will place you in front of a moving bus to cover their own errors- and he has had to develop his sixth sense to be able to sniff out the bad ones. Trusting his instincts has kept him in business for long and he wasn't about to start questioning it.

There was something he didn't like about Rick, and whether it was jealousy or there was actually something there, he'd keep it to himself if he wants to stay friends with Melissa.

He pulled up into the hotel's parking lot and Melissa spotted their rental.

"There, his car is over there."

"You see, I told you that you were just being paranoid. He probably just overslept. You can't deny that the weather is perfect for sleeping in."

She eased up a bit and smiled.

"Thank you, Matt."

"You're welcome."

"I'll see you at the church."

She hugged him briefly and got down from the car. Wrapping the coat Matt gave her tightly around herself to protect herself from the chill, she walked as fast as she could into the hotel. Alone in the elevator, she started thinking about the time she spent with Matt and how guilty she felt for the most part.

"I didn't do anything wrong." She muttered to herself. She had been saying the phrase over and over in her mind since they shared that hug. She tried to convince herself that it was just a hug, but she knew differently.

The elevator arrived on their floor and she rushed out. She knew that all her thoughts will vanish the moment he holds her.

She stopped midway from raising her hand to lift the knocker when she noticed the door was hanging slightly open. Her heartbeat picked up speed and it got so loud she could hear the pounding in her ears. With trepidation, she kicked the door open and started screaming immediately.

Her screams alerted one of the room cleaners and when she saw why Melissa was screaming, she immediately called the front desk, and they called 911. They tried to lead her away, but she wouldn't move, just stood by the entrance, staring at Rick's lifeless body.

Melissa felt as if she was having an out of body experience. When she kicked that door open and saw Rick lying in a pool of blood with the knife sticking out of his chest, it felt as if her very soul rose out of her body and started floating above her, observing the room, while her body just stood there with eyes that were open but not really seeing, a raw throat that can't make any more noises and legs that are rooted to the floor and can't move.

"Melissa." A voice called from very close to her. It sounded very familiar, but she couldn't tell who it belongs to.

"Melissa." The voice said again, gently and touched her arm. It was then she turned to look at the person.

"Matt?" she croaked, not believing he was really there. She didn't want to believe anything her eyes have seen since she opened the door to the hotel room.

"I got a call." He said gently, staring at her intently.

She wanted to ask who called him and how they knew to call him but she was too disconnected from her thoughts to piece the pieces together coherently so she just blinked slowly at him.

"I'm going to lead you away now, okay? You are currently in shock."

"Shock?"

"Yes, Mels. Can you walk or do you want me to carry you?"

"Walk?" she blinked slowly again and she heard Matt murmur a cuss to himself.

He lifted her like a baby and held her close to his chest. He carried her to another room and laid her gently on the bed and tucked her in.

"Do you want to sleep, Mels?"

"Sleep?"

"It's okay. I'll be here when you wake up."

Melissa drifted off, and had several dreams that had blood in it. She woke up with a start and jerked up in bed.

"Hey, hey. I'm here. You're safe." Matt said, coming to her side immediately.

She had dreamt that Rick had been stabbed and that she drowned in his blood. Her floating soul had returned to her at some point and the reality of what she had seen was finally settling in and she felt as if she had a crack on her forehead that was slowly spreading all over her body- she felt herself fall apart slowly, painfully.

"Is it real?" She asked Matt and the sadness she saw in her eyes was enough to confirm it.

It didn't start and end in her dream, he was really dead. Forever.

"I'm so sorry, Melissa. I am really sorry about this."

She took a deep breath. Then another. Then another until she started hyperventilating. Matt held her through it and didn't let go even when it subsided.

"It's not him. He can't be dead." She whispered, but Matt doesn't say anything.

A knock on the door and Jason came in looking like he hadn't slept in a week.

"Is it true?" He asked both of them and Matt nodded sadly.

"Jesus Christ." He ran his hands through his already tousled hair. On another day, Melissa would have laughed at his bird nest hair, but there would be no joy in the world for her for a long while. Maybe even forever.

"My God, Melissa." He walked over to the bed and sat on the other side. A thought crossed through her mind and she chuckled darkly. Both men looked at each other, then at her.

"What is it?" Matt asked.

"Look at us", she began, her voice sounding raw, "We ignore each other all these years and here we are, reunited by loss. Isn't that ironic?"

Matt and Jason look at each other again, but don't say anything. There was nothing to say.

"I want to see him." She said.

"Not yet. He just got taken away. The police want to question you. You'll be taken to see him afterwards."

"Dear God."

That's when the meltdown started.

Chapter Sixteen

Matt didn't return to see Melissa until several hours later. He left her with Jason to bury his father, and he returned to the hotel immediately after.

"How is she?" Jason was standing outside her door when he got off the elevator.

"Not good at all. She couldn't speak with the police; she was a fucking mess." Jason informed him.

"And you, how are you holding up? How was the funeral?"

"I don't know, man. I can't process that right now."

"I understand." Jason patted his shoulder and Matt smiled at him.

"Thanks, man. Did you pick anything up from the police? This whole thing is just strange. I can't remember the last time something like this happened here. It's all so fucking strange."

"I know, right? The already questioned me. Asked me where I was around 10 pm. That's the estimated time the crime was committed."

"The storm was still raging then."

"That's what I thought too, and from what I picked up, they are suspecting it's a suicide."

"That's even worse. He called Melissa earlier in the evening and was going to come pick her at mine. He couldn't have killed himself."

"They are just being lazy. Like you said, they have not had something like this in a while."

"I'll take care of it. Proper investigation must be carried out."

"He couldn't have killed himself."

The two men turned around and found Melissa standing behind them, looking like a very pale shadow of the girl Matt had dropped off earlier.

"Hey."

"How are you holding up?"

Melissa ignored both of them and started to go in the direction of the room she shared with Rick, and they didn't stop her.

She had a brief moment of déjà vu as she opened the door, except this time there was no pool of blood, and there no dead Rick on the floor. The room just like it did when they had first arrived. Rick had said something to the effect of not expecting small town Oklahoma to have a hotel this nice and she had told him not to be rude, even as she chuckled.

A sob caught in her throat, but she swallowed it and walked into inside. The smell of cleaning agents was overwhelming, but it couldn't completely cover the smell of blood. Melissa could sniff blood out like a hound, and she hated the smell. It was the main reason she didn't even think twice about going to med school when her career advisor mentioned it to her in high school.

She could smell the blood and she felt nauseated by it.

"Don't touch anything, Melissa. I don't think we're even supposed to be here." Jason cautioned. It was just as well, the nausea was getting stronger and bile was beginning to make its way up her throat.

"Okay." She left with them and Matt closed the door behind them.

"I already packed your things up, they are in the other room."

"Okay."

They both exchanged worried looks.

"Do you want to go on ride with us?" Matt offered, hoping the fresh air would help her a bit. To an extent, he understood what she was going through, but he also knew it was probably harder for her. Losing your husband a few days after getting married was definitely different from losing your old man.

"Okay."

She sat at the front with Matt, and Jason took the backseat. Matt saw just how tired Jason was from the rearview mirror.

"Are you okay, man? How did it go with Yolanda?"

Jason scrubbed at his face and sighed heavily.

"We're going our separate ways. She'll be going back to New York the moment she can get a flight."

"Shit. I'm sorry to hear that." Matt said.

"What happened between you guys?" Melissa asked from the front. She was looking out the window so they couldn't see her face.

"I'm an ass." Jason said in way of an answer and laughed shakily.

"According to her, I am better off marrying my virtual assistant, Eleanor than her because I pay her more attention."

"That's rough. You don't want to work it out? That sounds like something that can be worked on." Matt said.

"It can, but I'm not sure I want to."

"Oh?"

Jason turned to look at Melissa, not sure it was the right time to have that conversation.

"Please, talk about it if you want to. I could really use the distraction." She said and sighed deeply.

"Well, I have been a shitty boyfriend, if I'm being sincere. I'm so engrossed in my work it is crazy."

"You have always been a nerd." Matt teased and Melissa chuckled a bit.

"It's not that. According to her, I'm trying so hard to prove something that I have lost count of everything that matters." He said the words bitterly, not because he thought she was lying but because the truth wasn't something he wanted to be confronted with. But when she brought everything up it was as if she stripped him of everything he had covered himself with and kicked him into a room full of mirrors. He didn't like what he saw staring back at him. He didn't like it one bit.

"What are you trying to prove, Jason?" Matt asked.

"I'm not sure." He said weakly.

"I think you do." Melissa said in a small voice. She was still looking out the window, but the conversation was keeping her mind from spiraling.

Matt looked at Jason through the rearview mirror and their gaze met. Jason looked away immediately, and Matt did too.

"It's like I've been trying to change who I am, like I've been trying to change who I am from the boy from a small town to someone that people know. I spent so long living in the shadow of other people I told myself I never wanted to feel that way again. I might have lost myself while doing that.”

“If you are referring to us, you were never in our shadow, Jason.” Matt responded and Melissa nodded.

“It didn’t feel that way.”

“Jason, if you have allowed something you perceived rule the course of your life over these years then it’s totally your fault.” Her voice wasn’t hard, but even Matt winced a bit and he felt sorry for Jason.

“You are right, and coming back home opened my eyes to that. I have been living my life wrong and I just feel like a fucking idiot.”

No one said anything; there really wasn’t anything to say. They were all absorbed in their own thoughts, wrapped up in their own grief. There wasn’t anything to say.

Chapter Seventeen

Matt convinced the police into conducting a thorough investigation with regards to Rick's death and they were working on it but even after two weeks, they were not even slightly close to cracking the case.

Jason went back to New York a few days after the crime, but he promised to stay in touch with his friends this time around. Matt's father's will had been read before he left and on the will, he had stated that he hoped Matt would reunite with his friends. Only family had been present for the reading and Matt had not told either of them, but he was even more determined to stay in touch with them this time.

Hearing Jason promise to try on his own had felt to Matt as if a great weight had been lifted off his chest.

After two weeks, Melissa decided to return to LA. Matt tried to persuade her to stay longer, but she insisted that she had to go back to work. He understood the need to say busy, of course, but he didn't feel right about leaving her to return to LA alone.

"Do you have a friend you can stay with? Or would you go stay at your parents'?"

"I am not going to stay with my parents. And I'll be fine, really. My best friend Laura is in LA. I have not been able to reach her, but that usually happens. She sometimes forgets to charge her cellphone for weeks, and she doesn't have an answering machine."

"Is she 90?" Matt asked, perplexed that someone would refuse to get an answering machine in this age.

"No!" Melissa smiled a little at his expression and Matt returned the smile, glad that she could at least smile.

"I'll come visit, if that's fine by you."

"You don't have to."

"No, but I want to."

"I would love that. Thank you, Matt."

"I know this little reunion didn't happen under the best circumstances, but I'm really glad I have you guys again."

"You never lost me. Not for one minute."

He pulled her into a hug and held her while she cried a bit, not minding the strange looks people were giving them.

"See you around." She said as she made her way to check in.

****

The flight back home was harder than all the two weeks since Rick's death. She had travelled to Oklahoma with her head on her husband's chest, now she was flying with a cold feeling in a chest, and the only thing she had to rest her head on was the window.

She cried quietly all through the ride, and when one air hostess came to ask her if she was fine, she told her not to worry about her.

"Can I get you anything?" the hostess asked.

"No, thank you." She sniffed, dabbing at her cheeks with her hands.

"Actually, do you have any vodka?"

The hostess looked around and back at Melissa and whispered conspiratorially.

"We usually don't serve vodka, but you look like you could really use it. You won't tell anyone what you're drinking is vodka, will you?"

"No, I promise."

"Okay, I'll mix it with fruit juice. We don't want you getting drunk."

"Thank you very much."

The hostess returned with a tall glass along with some sandwiches, and a bottle of water.

"You should eat too."

"Thank you."

She went for the glass immediately. She had barely been eating since Rick's death and she knew she had lost considerable weight, must explain why the hostess thought she needed to eat.

Melissa nursed her drink and let her thoughts drift to her last moments with Rick as they have always done. There had been no indication that he was in trouble with any one that could want to kill him, or that he had any thoughts of taking his own life. Rick was too proud to take his own life and she had tried to explain that to the police when they had been trying to pass it off as a suicide.

Who could have killed him then?

That has been the thought that has been on her mind since she found out. He was very likable and he had his way with people. He was loved at his place of work and at the country club. Everyone loved Rick, but yet he was found with a knife in his chest that someone else clearly put there.

The whole thing made no sense to her, nothing made sense to her. The fact that she has to move on without any form of closure or even the slightest inclination as to why her husband was killed made everything impossibly harder. She sipped her drink slowly, not wanting it to finish before they arrive at Los Angeles.

She had told her parents and she had no doubt that her mother would be there to see her even though she had told them that she would be fine.

Her mother had taken it a step further and was waiting for her at the airport when she arrived. She had a placard with her name on it and for a few seconds, Melissa had been tempted to pretend not to see her and sneak away. But she felt incredibly lonely again where just a few weeks ago, she had her arms around someone, so she walked over to her mum let herself be pulled into a hug.

"My baby." Her mother planted several kisses on her face and pulled her into another hug.

"Come on, let's get you home. When last did you eat anything?"

"I can't remember." She had not touched the sandwiches on the plane.

"Have you been drinking?"

"Just a little."

"On an empty stomach?"

Melissa shrugged and her mother sighed.

"Come on, let's get you home."

She signaled for the potter to follow with her luggage and she held Melissa around the waist.

The ride home was quiet. Usually, her mother would attempt to talk to her about everyone she knew, but she left her to her thoughts and Melissa appreciated it.

"I'll stay with you for a while." Her mother announced when they were settled in.

"You don't have to, mother. I can take care of myself."

"That's bullshit and you know it. Look at you, you had people to look out for you and you hardly ate. I wonder what will happen if you're left alone. What will you do, uhn? Have a Cosmo for breakfast and Dirty Margarita for dinner every day?"

Melissa didn't deny it.

"Please, baby. I'll be more at peace knowing that you are safe and healthy. Please."

Melissa nodded once and her mother pulled her into another hug.

"I'm going to make you soup. Go change out of those clothes."

"I'm not hungry." She grumbled.

"It wasn't a request, Mel. You don't have to change if you don't want to, but you will eat."

"Yes, ma'am."

While her mum cooked, Melissa went to shower and change into something more comfortable than the jeans and leather jacket she was wearing.

"Can't say you don't look better." Her mother smiled warmly at her and passed her a large bowl of what was no doubt chili soup.

"Where did you get the ingredients you used for this?" she asked, eyeing the soup suspiciously.

"Oh, I brought it from home, I only popped it into the microwave. I didn't think you'd have changed."

"Good thinking." Melissa chuckled.

"Eat, Melissa. Please, baby."

Melissa sighed, but she dug her spoon into the soup and started eating. In ten minutes, she was done eating and her mother looked very relieved.

"Do you want more? Or you want some cake? Cookies?"

"Did you bring everything in your kitchen here?"

"Well, your father will not starve, if that's what you're concerned about. Let me give you a slice of this lemon curd cake I baked, you'll love it."

Before Melissa could protest, a large piece of cake was placed in front of her. Her mother served a slice for herself as well, along with chocolate ice cream she no doubt found in her refrigerator.

"This is so good, mother. Christ." Melissa groaned at the deliciousness of the cake in her mouth.

"Told ya." Her mother smiled smugly.

"How didn't I get any of the cooking spirit from you? I'm totally useless in the kitchen."

"We have some time on our hands now, so I could show you some things."

"I'm going back to work, mother." There was a challenge in Melissa's eyes, but her mother wasn't fazed by it.

"Do you honestly think you are fit to work? Think about it, Melissa. Do you think you can go back to work and be fully on top of your game?"

She looked away from her mother and continued eating.

"That's what I thought."

They ate in silence for a while until she caught her mum staring at her rings. She had not been able to bear taking them off. They were a bitter reminder of what she had lost, but they were also the last piece she had of him.

"How are you doing, sweetie?"

"How do you think?"

"Fair enough. How was the funeral? Did Jason attend?"

"Yes, he did. I quite enjoyed my time with Matt and Jason. At least, the little time I spent with them before the incident happened."

"Will you stay in touch with them now?" Her mother knew all about what happened between them. She started talking to her mother about her life in her final year in high school, and she hadn't stopped since then. Over the years, she had tried to convince her to reconnect with her old friends but she always told her things were better the way they were.

"Yes, I guess so. We've been acting like children, and we are all adults now."

"I'm glad. Is there any progress with Rick's case?"

"No. They have hit a dead end. I suspect that they might abandon it."

"That's ridiculous."

"Tell me about it."

"Do you want me to inform your father? He can pull some strings and ensure that they continue investigating the case."

"No need for that." She suddenly felt all the life drain out of her as a wave of tiredness hit her. "I just want to put this all behind me, really."

"It's okay, baby. One day at a time."

One day at a time.

Melissa murmured the words to herself. It was going to become her new mantra.

"I'm going to go lay down now."

"That's fine, I'll be here when you wake up."

Melissa looked at her sadly, but she didn't say anything. She wasn't certain about anything anymore. She had expected to meet Rick back at the hotel, instead he was dead. Another huge part of working through grief was guilt. No matter what Matt said, she was still going to blame herself a bit for Rick's death.

If she hadn't asked him to follow her to Oklahoma, he'd probably still be alive and he'd be the one feeding her ice cream and cake and not her mother.

"You can't think like that." Matt had said. "If it works that way, then I might as well shoulder the blame because I asked you out here in the first place. We still don't know the circumstances behind his death, so we can't make any assumptions. If you continue thinking that way, you'll not heal. Please."

It made sense when he said the words, but she goes back and forth between rational thinking and the guilt, but for the most part, the guilt pulled harder at her.

Chapter Eighteen

After two weeks of not being able to reach Laura and not hearing anything from her, Melissa decided to go to her house. She had tried to reach her at her workplace and had been told that she stopped working for them about three months ago. Melissa didn't know what to say to that, but a very bad feeling took root in her heart and she didn't know how else to shake it.

"Do you want me to come with you?" Her mother asked. If she absolutely had to admit it, having her mother around had helped her a great deal. But no one was asking her to admit it, so she wasn't going to before the woman got any ideas and decides to stay for much longer.

"No, mother. It's fine. I'll be back soon."

"Be safe, okay?"

"I promise."

Her mother watched her leave with worry in her eyes and Melissa felt a warm feeling in her chest.

Laura's house looked abandoned, for lack of a better word. Melissa found the spare key she keeps under her 'You Shall Not Pass' foot mat and let herself into the house with it. The same feeling of trepidation she felt when she found Rick's body overtook her body and she felt the strong urge to go back, lock the door and drive back home and pretend she never came looking for Laura at all. But, she needed to know what was going on with her or her mind would not be at peace. It occurred to her that she could just call the police, but what would she say? So she steeled herself and entered the house.

There was not a single thing out of place in the house. She checked the two rooms, the bathrooms, kitchen, study, everywhere, but there was no sign of Laura. The only thing that seemed out of place was the thin layer of dust that covered the furniture.

"Where the hell are you, Laura?" she said to the empty house.

A note sticking out from underneath her phone caught her attention and she went to retrieve it. It had two words on it, but those words threw her world out of focus for a few seconds.

"CALL RICK!"

She took the note with her as she stumbled out of her house, even more confused than when she entered.

"Mum." She called the moment she walked in, eager to share what she found with someone. She felt as if her head was going to explode if she doesn't talk to someone about what she had seen. It made no sense to her, of course, but she needed to talk to someone nonetheless.

"In here." Her mother called from the kitchen, and Melissa went there straight without taking off her coat or dropping her bag.

"Mum you'll not believe…" she trailed off when she saw Matt sitting on one of the kitchen chairs, cookie in hand and looking as if it was normal for her to walk into her kitchen and find him there. He even waved cheerfully at her.

"Matt?" she questioned dumbly.

Matt looked down at his hands, felt his face then said, "Yup. I should hope so." That earned a hearty laughter from her mum and she chuckled a bit.

"What are you doing here?" When she gave him her address before she left Oklahoma, she didn't think he'd be paying her a visit soon.

"I was in town for business and I decided to stop by to say hello." His eyes took her in from head to toe, and as if satisfied with what he saw, he looked back up at her face with a smile on his face.

"You didn't really come here for business, did you?" she said flatly.

"I did, I swear it."

"I'll leave you kids to it. It was nice to see you again, Matt."

"It was nice to see you too, ma'am. And your cookies are as awesome as I remember them to be."

They waited until they couldn't hear her footsteps anymore before they started talking.

"We need to talk." Matt said seriously, all the humor in his voice completely faded away.

"Do I need to be seated for this?" she asked as her heart rate picked up again. Without waiting for an answer, she sat down on the chair her mother vacated.

"What's going on, Matt? Did the police find something?"

"No, I'm afraid there is nothing new on that end. They seem to have reached a dead end. I'm sorry."

"What's going on then?"

"Well, it's about Rick."

"I kind of figured that out, but you said the police didn't find anything yet."

"No, I'm not talking about his death. I'm talking about Rick himself."

"Oh."

"I know you told me to behave, but I have learned to trust my instinct. It has never lied to me, and I didn't think it was lying to me when I felt off about Rick."

"Where are you going with this?"

"Well, I kind of started asking around about him."

"What do you mean by you started asking around? Who did you ask?" She regarded him curiously.

"Okay, fine. I hired a private detective. The police didn't have anything and I couldn't stand seeing you this way."

"And your instinct was telling you there's something wrong with him." She said, but it sounded a lot like an accusation.

"Please, just hear me out before you close your mind off to what I have to say." He pleaded.

"Okay." She crossed her hands over her chest.

"As I was saying, I got a private detective and what he came back with blew my mind. I had to come show you immediately because you might be in a lot of trouble."

"What kind of trouble?" A cold shiver went down her spine as she remembered the note she found at Laura's.

"Before I show you what I have, tell me how you met him."

"I met him four years ago, we got introduced by my best friend, Laura."

He produced a file from his bag, opened it and brought out a picture.

"Is this her?" he asked.

A large, glossy image of Laura stared back at her. Her hair was different- short and red, and she had a nose ring on, but it was most certainly her.

"Yes." She said in a whisper.

"I thought as much."

"Matt, what is going on?"

"Okay, what I'm going to show you now is going to change a lot of things for you, but I promise you that we'll fix it."

"Just give me the folder." She stretched her hand out for it and he handed it over wordlessly.

Her primary instinct was to open it and tear through it immediately, but she held back. If someone tell you that something is going to change your life, and not in a good way, no matter how curious you are, you kind of want to take a few moments to savor the moments before your world falls apart.

Slowly, she opened the file and started going through the content. Every line she read struck her like a blow to the heart, and by the time she was done, she was certain that her life was over.

How is it possible that within a few moments, you discover that almost everything that you hold dear was a well-crafted lie and your life is one huge fat lie, and that's not even the worst part. The worst part is that you were being played like a puppet in your own life and you didn't even know. Naturally, your mind tries to reject what it read to protect you, because there is no way you could have been that blinded. You reject it.

"This is not true. There is no way this is true." She shook her head vigorously, trying to convince her mind to reject what she read.

"It is, Mels and I think that a part of you knows it. That's the only way this whole thing makes sense."

"Are you trying to tell me that Rick was only playing an act when he was with me and that he didn't love me?"

"I'm sorry." Matt said, not meeting her gaze.

Melissa started hyperventilating and Matt rushed to her side.

"Deep breaths. Deep breaths." He rubbed her back and made soothing sounds while she tried to get her breathing under control.

"Why, Matt? I never hurt anyone. Why do I have such bad luck?"

"It's not you. It's not your fault this happened. Good people get hurt all the time by no fault of theirs."

"That's not all." Matt said when she calmed down.

"No, of course it's not." She laughed bitterly.

"Melissa?"

"It's okay. Tell me."

"Well, you might be at risk of going to jail." He said quietly. That was the hardest part of the whole thing.

"What do you mean?"

He brought out another file, a smaller one this time, but he doesn't give it to her.

"The main reason Rick went through all that is so as to divest you of your money."

"I figured, but that's the part that makes no sense. He has a great job and he has never asked me for money. So I don't understand any of this."

"From what Richard discovered, he had never been with any of his victims longer than a year before doing what he came for and leaving."

"I've known him for four years. Perhaps this is different." She hated the hope in her voice. She hated how foolish she felt, and she hated the fact that he was dead and she couldn't ask him about any of this. The look on Matt's face at her hope made her feel even more foolish.

"No, Mels. He started out to do the same thing, but we have strong reasons to think he was waiting for a bigger payout. You're the wealthiest of his victims so far."

"But I'm not even wealthy!"

"You are signatory to a wealthy company."

Her features went completely stiff.

"What do you mean?"

"My theory is that he has found a way to steal the company's money."

"How can he do that? He doesn't have access to…" her voice trailed off as the pieces fell into place before her eyes.

"Oh God." She breathed and started shivering. Matt hurried to fetch his jacket and draped it over her shoulder.

"What is it?"

"We are married."

"I know. What does that imply?"

"It means that we are bound legally and technically my share of the company belongs to him as well, and his properties belong to me too. I don't understand it fully, but it means he can use my name to commit a crime. Also, he took a lot of interest in my work. He always wanted to know all the details and I told him everything he asked. But I didn't suspect anything because he took a lot of interest in all aspects of my life. The man knew everything about me, and it was one of the things I loved the most about him. God, I am so foolish!"

"It's okay. We can fix this."

"Fix? We don't even know what is wrong. We don't know what he did or if he did anything."

"He didn't have his laptop in Oklahoma, do you know where it is?"

"Yeah, it's back at his. He said he didn't want to take work with him so that he'd be fully present for me."

"Let's go get it."

"Okay. Matt, do you think she killed him?"

She had been trying not to think about Laura's involvement in this whole thing. There would be a time, perhaps later when she had reached a point of stability and she wasn't in any trouble when she would bring that particular case file out and examine it. But it wasn't now. Now, she was doing her best not to lose her mind and she could only deal with one thing at a time.

"I don't know, but she's our only suspect now."

"Shouldn't we tell the police what we know?"

"We will after we are sure that you are not in any kind of trouble."

"Okay."

"One more thing." Melissa looked at him dejectedly and his heart broke even more. He hated to be the one bringing her this amount of bad news, but it had to be done, and he would rather be the one to do it than have a stranger break the news to her.

"I called Jason. He'll be flying down here today."

"What?"

"Please don't get mad, but we can't do it alone, and we might need to hack into his computer, or something. We need as much help as we can get and I didn't think you'd want me to involve a stranger."

All the air left her sail. He had a point, of course.

"Let's go."

The drive to his house was agonizing. She hadn't been there since she got back to LA out of grief, but now, she was feeling more than grief. Her feelings were a cocktail of grief, anger, betrayal, confusion, more grief and a deep sadness. All she wanted to do was curl up into a ball somewhere and cry but instead, she was driving to the house of perhaps the most despicable human she ever had the ill fortune of meeting.

Rick's house looked like a tornado happened inside it. On the outside, everything looked normal, but the inside was completely chaotic.

"Oh my God." She whispered and Matt whistled loudly.

Whoever searched his apartment was very thorough as they didn't leave any table unturned- literally and figuratively.

"I don't think we'll find his laptop here." Matt said.

"Does he have a safe here or a safety deposit box?"

"He has a home safe, but I have never seen what's inside, neither do I know the password."

"I'll take care of that. Just show me the safe."

She took him to the basement where the safe was concealed behind a bookshelf. She pulled out a book and the shelf opened up to reveal a safe. Matt chuckled darkly.

"What?"

"For such a well concealed safe, it uses the most basic security system."

"Can you get it open?"

"I'll pop it open like a soda can." He cracked his knuckles and stepped towards the safe. Melissa watched him work, and after a few minutes, the safe opened.

"That was fast. How did you do that?"

"It's easy. I just had to override the system. It's the easiest safe to crack like I said."

"What's inside?" she asked, stepping closer to him.

"It's dark in there. Can you get me a flashlight, please?" Melissa found one in the basement.

"Here goes nothing."

They found passports to different countries, different foreign currencies, a lot of cash and a laptop."

"Viola."

"That's not his laptop." Melissa said.

"No. That's not the laptop you know. This is probably the one we are looking for, however."

"And probably what the person that wrecked the house was looking for." She mused.

"Yup."

Matt took the laptop and closed the safe. They returned the shelf to its place and left the house.

"Yesterday, I was mourning the love of my life."

"Today, I discovered he was a wrecking ball that was pushed into my life by a person I thought was my best friend. Life does come at you fast, doesn't it?"

"Melissa, don't feel sorry for yourself. Don't let yourself be the victim here."

"But I am the victim."

"No, we are going to turn this around and you'll be a survivor."

When they got back to the house, Jason was waiting for them, and her mother was doting over him. It felt like a déjà vu moment.

"Hey, Mels." Jason hugged her and she felt one of her fractured piece heal up.

"I'm so sorry about everything. We'll do all we can to help out, you have nothing to worry about."

"What's going on?" Melissa's mother asked, looking from Matt to Jason and back to Melissa.

"Turns out Rick was a fraud and he and Laura were working together to defraud me. We don't know the extent of their plans, but we are about to find out."

"What are you talking about?'

Wordlessly, she handed her mother the file Matt had given her earlier.

"Oh, what fresh hell." Her mother exclaimed.

"This can't be real."

"It is, mum. We just came back from his place and there are some really incriminating evidences there."

"What are we going to do now?" she asked, looking alarmingly pale.

"It's fine. We'll take care of it. Could you hook us up with another batch of those cookies, please?"

"Okay, I can do that." She said faintly.

"Mum?"

"Yes, honey?"

"Could you not mention a word of this to dad, please? He has a tendency to overreact and I don't need that right now."

"Okay. I promise."

"Thanks, mum."

"Did you get the laptop?" Jason asked when they moved to the study.

"Yup."

"Great."

Matt handed it to him and in a few seconds, he had hacked into it.

"It baffles me how you guys can just break into stuff. Jason, are you a software developer or a hacker?" she needed to distract herself and discovering these new things about her friends was distracting enough.

"I can do both." He winked at her. "The way I figure it, why be one thing when you can be several?"

"Hear hear." Matt said. He had left briefly and returned with three glasses and a bottle of whiskey.

"Looks like someone grew up into a young woman that knows her liquor." Matt said in appreciation.

"I have Rick to thank for that." She said sadly and Matt rolled his eyes.

"At least he was useful for something."

He poured whisky for all of them and joined Jason by the computer.

"Did you find anything?"

"Just more proof that this guy was a real bastard, but nothing that concerns Melissa yet."

"Keep looking, I'm sure you'll find something."

"Yes, boss." Jason said drily and rolled his eyes at Matt.

"Eleanor, could you cancel the rest of my plans for today? This is going to take a while."

Matt and Melissa turned a curious gaze at him.

"Roger that, boss." Eleanor said through his smart watch.

"Jason, why is your Siri named Eleanor?" Melissa asked.

"That's because I'm not Siri." The voice said through Jason's wristwatch.

"Hello, Matt. Hello, Melissa. My name is Eleanor, it's nice to meet you."

Matt and Melissa stared at his wristwatch, utterly stupefied. Without even breaking his flow, Jason said, "It is rude not to say 'hi' back, you know?"

"Hi."

"Hi."

Matt and Melissa said in unison and Jason chuckled, enjoying their reaction. It never got old.

"That's Eleanor, my virtual personal assistant. She's like Siri, but a more intelligent version. Way more intelligent."

"Did you build her?" Melissa asked, coming closer.

"Yup."

"Dude, that is so cool!"

"I know, right? She makes my life easier."

"Why is she not on the market then? You'll make a shit load of money from it, you know?"

"I know." Jason shrugged, "But I like being the only person that has something."

"Remember when he had that toy race car and then he wouldn't play with it again when Emily Lauren got the same type." Matt said and Melissa burst into uncontrollable laughter.

"Sure, laugh." Jason said, but he was laughing himself.

"Oh, shit." Jason said after a while, removing his hands from the keyboard as if had suddenly caught on fire.

"What? What did you find?" Matt and Melissa flanked him on both sides.

"What am I looking at?" Melissa asked, confused by the numbers she was seeing on the keyboard.

"You know how we weren't sure how he was trying to rob you, or the extent of whatever plans he might have set in motion?"

"Yes?" They both intoned, still very confused.

"Well, the answer is everything."

"Everything of what?"

"Your father's company. He's making you milk it for all its worth."

"Oh my God. Oh my God. I need to sit down."

Matt peered closer at the screen.

"If this gets out, she's going to go to jail. There is no way to prove that she didn't authorize it."

"I know, and that's what makes it worse."

"What are we going to do?"

"We have to tell the police now. We need to inform someone before they find out at the company. I'll never recover from this."

"You'll never recover from it if you tell the police. This guy did a clean job. The only fingerprints he left are yours and it can and probably will be traced back to you."

"So, I'm screwed. Is that what you're saying? That I should just sit and wait for whichever one of my choices will ruin me?" Her voice had reached a point of hysteria and she felt like she was having a complete mental breakdown.

"No, that's not what I'm saying." Jason said. "I have a suggestion, but it's not in any way ethical."

Matt had pulled Melissa to him and was holding her tightly. "What do you suggest?"

"Well, he laundered all the money out to a bank in Switzerland. I have all the bank details. I can hack into that account and steal all that money and send it back to your company's account."

"You can do that?" Matt asked incredulously.

"I built software for use in Wall Street; this is an, erm, added benefit they don't know about."

"Damn."

"How do manage to keep yourself on the good path?"

"By building sentient virtual assistants that no one else has."

"The bank will know, won't they?" Melissa asked quietly. "They'll know that they have lost money, especially that kind of money. Won't they come looking for it?"

"They will."

Chapter Nineteen

Melissa stared at him as if he has suddenly developed a second head.

"What happens when they do, Jason?" she asked slowly as if she were talking to a child.

"I'll create a fake account and drop the money there for a while before transferring it back to where it originally belongs. They will be able to trace it to the fake account, but the trace will vanish from there."

"In whose name will the account be in?" Matt asked.

"What happens when the bank reports the theft? It will still make me look bad."

"Don't worry about that, I will change all the details. Your name will not appear anywhere. And the way I see it, since Rick is dead, and your company's money is back where it belongs, there will be no one to miss the money that was stolen. The bank will rather let the case die than cause any trouble for themselves. The fake account is just in case someone decides to look."

"That sounds perfect." Matt grinned.

"This is too much for me to take in. There are just so many things that could go wrong."

Jason turned to face her completely. "Melissa, listen to me. I am very good at what I do and if I believe in nothing else, I believe in myself completely. This is the only way we can get you out of trouble. If we try to do the legally correct thing, you might end up going to prison. Please, let me fix this, okay?"

"Okay."

Jason turned back to face the computer and Matt joined him.

"I'm going to go lay down for a bit." Melissa announced after a while and left the study before either of them could respond.

When she woke up, it felt as if she had been asleep for an entire year. In fact, she woke up with a start, slightly unaware of where she was. After a few minutes of blinking in the dark, it all came back to her. Completely exhausted, she dragged herself out of bed and went in search of her friends.

She caught the time on her way, and saw she had been asleep for almost four hours. She remembered reading once that some people used sleep as a form of coping mechanism from psychological pain.

"Hey, sleepy head." Matt greeted her when she entered the study. He was reclining on one of her chairs, a cup of coffee in hand. In fact, the whole room smelled like coffee, whiskey and cookies.

"Have you guys been here since?"

"Yup. Jason is like a work machine, I'm here for moral support and your mum has been fueling us with coffee and cookies."

"Sounds like fun." She muttered.

"Hi, Jace." She had not used her nickname for him in a really long time, but it didn't sound strange when she did.

"Hey, Mels. Sleep good?"

She shrugged.

"You should both get some rest. We don't have to finish this today, do we?"

"Yes." Both Matt and Jason intoned.

"You never can tell when someone will find out that all the company's money is gone. We need to reverse everything as soon as possible." He responded without looking up from the screen.

"Thank you guys for doing this. I don't even have enough words to tell you how much means to me." And it's true; she didn't know where to begin thanking them from. One day she thought she had it all- the perfect man, a best friend she adores, a great job and an amazing life, and the next day, her perfect man dies and she finds out later that he's a fraud, and her best friend might have killed him, her job is threatened and her life is turned upside down. Melissa was learning very fast that often times, the place you desperately try to run from is truly your home, and the people you desperately try to forget are the ones that will risk their necks to save you.

"It's nothing." Jason said, even though she could see the strain in his features.

It wasn't nothing. It was everything and more and her heart swelled with love for these boys she had shared a lot of her milestones with as a child and teenager.

"I love you guys so fucking much. I'm sorry I came between you guys and ruined our friendship. I truly am sorry and I hope we can stay friends for real this time." She said, suddenly overcome by emotions.

"What are you talking about?" Jason asked.

"I made the first move. If I didn't do that, none of that shit would have happened and maybe we wouldn't have missed out ten years of one another's life."

"It's alright. I didn't react well either. I acted like you owed me something. I'm sorry." Jason turned to Matt, "And I'm sorry for how I acted then, and how I acted all the times you tried to reach out. I truly am."

"It's all good. And I'm sorry I broke your trust and making you feel like you weren't good enough for her. I respected you back then, man. And I still do now. You have always been one hell of a person."

"Awww." Melissa's mother cooed from the door to the study. "Look at you guys making up and stuff. I'm so proud of you kids!"

"Mum!" Melissa sniffed, slightly embarrassed.

They three of them smiled at one another and Jason went back to work.

"I'm done." Jason announced well past midnight.

"You are?" Matt sat up- he had been dozing slightly.

"Yup."

"I'm not going to jail?"

"Not for a crime you didn't commit, no."

"Oh God."

And then she started crying again.

****

"I have dreamed about this for a very long time." Matt said when she woke up. He was looking at her like she was food and he couldn't wait to gobble her up.

"Oh yeah?" she stretched lazily, and he took that opportunity to kiss her exposed throat.

It was a year after the incident and Melissa's life had taken on a sense of normality again. The police never did solve the case of Rick's death and Laura was arrested for drug trafficking in Dubai. When Jason gave her the news, she had smiled a little to herself, and immediately felt guilty for her reaction.

It took a lot of work, but she closed the chapter of her life that featured Laura and Rick for good. When Matt asked her out on a date and they kissed that night in the rain, it felt right. It felt as if the universe had finally aligned perfectly for her and everything was as it's supposed to be. It felt like the most natural thing in the world.

Waking up next to him in his home in Oklahoma on a Monday morning instead of being at work in LA also felt like the most natural thing in the world. In fact, if it involves Matt, then the moment is perfect.

"Yeah."

"What exactly did you see in this dream?"

"A certain blue eyed blonde with the most perfect everything I have ever seen was on my bed, stretching and purring like a satisfied kitten. In my dream, I told her that I love her and she smiled at me and said she loves me too."

That woke Melissa up faster.

"You love me?" they had been dating, but they were yet to make any promises to each other, or even use the L-word.

"To tiny pieces. I love you so much it is sometimes difficult to breathe when I think about it. I have loved you since I was 15, Mels, and if you let me I will love you till I'm old and grey."

Melissa was at a loss for words. She has had a lot of guys profess their love to her and she has said it back on several occasions. But this time was different. Everything about being with Matt was different.

"You don't have to say it back now; I just wanted you to know." She nodded, fighting hard to hold the tears in.

"Come on, let's go get dressed. If we are late, Jason will chew our ears off." Matt offered a hand to help her to her feet.

"When did he get so bossy?" Melissa grumbled.

"If you can do half the things that dude can do, you'll be bossy too."

"That's true, you have a point."

****

"I should probably thank all the gods in Olympus that you two deemed it fit to leave your bed to come see me." Jason grumbled when Matt and Melissa finally joined him at the park. They had decided to go out for breakfast together before Jason and Melissa left Oklahoma. They had both been around for their high school reunion and they had decided to stay a while longer.

"We're sorry, Jace."

"No, you are not. You'll probably do the same thing again."

"We said we're sorry, man. Come on, let's go."

They enjoyed the leisurely walk to the restaurant that used to be their favorite place to eat and hangout when they were younger.

"Do you think the food there will still be as nice?" Jason asked.

"I should hope so; else this will be a total bust." Melissa responded.

"God, I have so missed their burger! Nothing in LA compares to their burger."

It looked as if they stepped back in time when they walked into the restaurant. They stood very still, waiting to see if Natasha would pass in her cute apron and tiny skirt.

"Did anyone else feel as if they time travelled?" Melissa asked and the guys nodded beside her.

"Did anything here change at all?" Jason marveled, looking at the plaid tablecloths.

"Look," Matt pointed. "Our spot is empty."

They hurried over there and sighed in contentment as they took their seats.

"This feels so good. Is going to eat at a restaurant supposed to feel this good?" Melissa moaned.

"If it's a crime, I absolutely do not mind being arrested for it." Matt added and Jason chuckled.

A teenage girl in a cute apron came to take their order. She had a nametag on her chest that said 'TASHA'.

The group exchanged a loaded look and burst into laughter.

"Erm, should I come back?" Tasha asked.

"No, it's fine." Jason said. "I will have the chef's special" he said without looking at the menu and Matt and Melissa stared at him, dumbfounded.

"What? I have always wanted to try the chef's special."

214